GET OFF YOUR HIGH HORSE

CYNTHIA TERELST

ISBN: 978-0-6487294-2-6

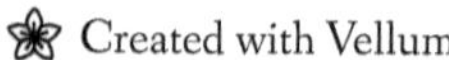 Created with Vellum

Thank you to those who shared their knowledge about horses and polo - Cheneya, Kate and Tina. The extra details I was able to add made the story come to life.

Thank you to Britney for allowing me to use your beautiful children as inspiration for Frankie's nieces and nephews.

KEEP IN TOUCH

To be notified of future releases, and to keep up to date with other news, please join my newsletter.

https://www.subscribepage.com/p9p9yo

CHAPTER ONE

Frankie

Ruby shifted her weight beside me and leant her 500 kg against my shoulder. Of course, it wasn't all of her weight. If it was, I'd be flat on the ground. Her warmth seeped through me. Turning my nose into her neck, I breathed in deep. I closed my eyes and let the smell of hay and horse seep into my senses. That smell would always be a cure for me; it could take my unsettled mind and set me straight.

Ruby moved her head to the right. I opened my eyes and followed suit. The polo players were at the other end of the field, the action amplifying as they approached the goals. The spectators' voices matched the intensity. Sebastian, one of our international riders, stood in his stirrups, giving himself more manoeuvrability, and intercepted the ball. He looked ahead. There was no one to pass it to. He hit it anyway. The connection of mallet on ball was deep and satisfying when Sebastian whacked it towards the goal at the opposite end of the field. The horses thundered across the grass in pursuit.

I loved the polo grounds here. We were right on the edge of the suburbs of Brisbane, but you wouldn't know that the capital city lay 35 kilometres away. Trees and undulating land surrounded the wide-open fields. The peacefulness reminded me of home.

Ruby moved her head, following the players' movements. Her body was relaxed. Her ears were pointed forward, twitching at the sounds from the field. Her eyes were bright and alert. She was watching, thinking, ready and eager to join as soon as it was her turn.

Sebastian may be a conceited royal, but he sure could ride, whether his butt was in the saddle or not. I smiled, thinking about what Amanda would often say: 'Frankie, that man has an arse anyone would be happy to grab'. As much as I hated to admit it, she was right. And it was just as good to look at. As was the rest of him with his sun-bleached brown hair, warm brown eyes and tanned features. But good looks and money weren't everything. And they certainly were not my thing.

Toro, whose lead rope I held in my other hand, was moving his feet in eagerness. While Ruby was calm, he was a ball of energy. His movements intensified, responding to the action on the field. Smiling at him, I tugged at his lead rope to get his attention, to remind him where he was and that he needed to settle. His response was instant. His feet stilled. He let out a long, drawn-out breath and licked his lips.

"Good boy," I said, reaching up to give him a pat.

Sebastian chased the ball down and hit it towards Andrew, one of the amateurs on our team. He had rolled up to the game in his Porsche fifteen minutes before we were due to start: barely enough time to ensure he was ready and learnt the game plan. I'd peeked at Sebastian and Juan, our two professional players, during the team meeting to gauge their reaction. They both had clenched jaws. When Sebastian had addressed Andrew, his voice was tight. At least his royal, good looking arse, took the game seriously.

Andrew and Juan were in the forward half waiting for the ball. Sebastian had passed the ball slowly, allowing Juan to draw the opposition playing on him away from the play, leaving Andrew and the goal open. If Andrew had missed the pass, Juan could have picked it up with ease. That's the difference between a good player and a great player: great players can think of multiple strategies at once. But Sebastian's pass was so precise there was no way Andrew could have missed the ball. Sebastian galloped around the outside into position to score a goal if Andrew passed it to him. In a professional game Andrew would have. Because in a professional game, it is about team success, not personal glory.

Andrew's mallet swung through the air and struck the ball. I cringed when the mallet followed through and struck his horse's leg. That was exactly why we put jump boots on the horses, in particular the ones the amateurs rode. They acted like shin guards in hockey or soccer.

The ball flew through the air. An opposition player galloped from left of field. For every 30cm the ball got closer to the goal, the rider gained a metre. Closer. Closer. I held my breath. It was like the ball was moving in molasses.

The opposition closed the distance. The ball was so close. He got closer. He lifted his mallet into the air to strike the ball, to prevent the goal and move the ball out of the attack zone. It made no purchase. The ball floated through the goals.

The crowd erupted. Andrew stood in his stirrups and cantered around beating his chest and pointing to himself like he was the be all and end all. I was surprised he didn't pull his shirt off like a soccer player who had kicked a goal in the World Cup. The other three players on our team came together and gave each other high fives.

Rolling my eyes at Andrew's antics, I patted Ruby and Toro. "It will be your turn soon. There's only a couple of minutes left in this chukka."

Sebastian and Andrew trotted past on their way to the next play. Andrew stopped and indicated to Ruby, "I don't want that horse."

"You don't want Ruby?"

"No, I want a faster horse."

He couldn't be serious. There were less than two minutes left in the period and he wanted to do a horse change? To a faster horse? Ruby was one of the fastest we had. As an off the track thoroughbred, she had great acceleration and speed. I bit my tongue but I'm sure my face said it all.

"Look at her. She's ready to fall asleep."

Idiot. I couldn't formulate words. Well, none that wouldn't get me in trouble. Instead, I nodded. Sebastian was tight lipped as he watched the exchange. The way he moved in his saddle I knew he was itching to say something. He didn't get the chance. Andrew spun and rode back to the game. Sebastian opened his mouth, but I turned away.

Being a polo groom was a thankless job sometimes. Especially when you had to deal with the Andrew's of the world. I took the phone out of my pocket and called Amanda who was down at the horse truck.

"Can you saddle Brutus and bring him up, please?"

"Why? What's happened?" Her voice was tight with concern.

"Andrew decided he doesn't want to ride Ruby."

Amanda was moving around. She would have tucked the phone into her bra and put it on loud speaker so she could use two hands. Knowing she had less than five minutes between chukkas to have Brutus ready, she'd be moving at top speed. She had to get his gear on and get him up here within that time. She'd be pushing shit uphill.

"Why?" she asked.

"Not fast enough, apparently."

"What a dick."

Her breathing was more laboured and I pictured her crouching to wrap Brutus's legs in bandages. Her blonde plait would have fallen over her shoulder. I pushed my ponytail back in response.

"Make sure you put the jump boots on. He whacked his horse at least once that I saw."

The bell signalling the end of the chukka sounded behind me. I put my phone in my breast pocket as the riders came over. Juan and Doug headed to our other groom. Breathing in, I prepared myself, and prayed Amanda would be done in time. I imagined her putting on the bridle and breast plate with head check attached. Amanda's fingers were nimble and she was always calm under pressure; the buckles would pose no problem for her.

Our riders were closer. I prepared for Sebastian to change horses. It was usually a fluid move from one horse to another. No need to hop off when time was of the essence. Instead he swung his leg and dismounted. Amanda would be putting the saddle pad and saddle on and connecting all the pieces together.

"Where's my horse?" Andrew demanded.

"Coming."

He jumped down and shoved the reins towards me. So, I was holding three horses, soon to be four, because Sebastian moved towards me. It wouldn't be a problem; they were all well behaved. But our rules were that we could only hold two at a game for safety reasons. Horses are flight animals and could be unpredictable.

"We need to get back on the field," Andrew said, pointedly.

"I'm aware of that."

Where was Amanda? I hoped she was close.

"Here, give me Toro," Sebastian said, reaching for the reins. For months his posh voice had grated on me, but not this time.

"Thank you." I gave him a small smile. At least I wasn't surrounded by jerks: just one.

"How much longer?" Andrew, the arsewipe, again.

"Here we are," Amanda called out in a fake cheery voice. She held Brutus while Andrew mounted. Without a word, he turned and rode away.

"Great job getting Brutus ready in such short time," Sebastian said. Before mounting Toro, he made sure his polo shirt was tucked in. I didn't need to look at Amanda to know she'd be enjoying the view. His breeches hugged his legs and his broad shoulders were accentuated when he drew himself up tall to tuck his shirt in.

He gave Ruby a pat as the bell sounded. Mounting Toro, he gave us a quick smile and rode away.

"Andrew's such a dick," Amanda said. "I can't believe he was so rude to you."

She would have heard it all through the phone in my pocket.

"Lucky you got here when you did. I was about to lose my shit."

She squeezed my arm. "One more season."

"One more season."

We walked back to the truck together. When we got there, I rested my head against Ruby's, our brown hair blending together, and rubbed her cheek. "Sorry, Andrew is such an arsehole," I said to her.

Her relaxed breathing helped slow the blood pumping through my veins. Giving her a final pat before tying her to the truck, I made my way back to the field with two horses in tow. I needed to be there in case one of the players broke a mallet or needed an emergency horse change. Not only that, though. I liked to see how the horses were performing to understand if they needed developmental training in a certain area. And if I saw they got a heavy bump from a horse or a hit from a mallet, I would know if they needed special attention in the days to come. Maybe light exercise or a massage.

I found it hard sometimes, thinking I had only one more season with these horses. Even though I would miss them, I wouldn't miss everything about polo. I wouldn't miss how some of the riders treated the horses like a commodity. How they had no care when they rode recklessly or hit a horse with their mallet. I wouldn't miss the pretentiousness of some players and how they would treat me and the other staff. If my dad had seen me behave like that, he would have given me a swift kick up the arse. Maybe that's what some of these high rollers needed.

When I got home, I wouldn't need to worry about this

world anymore. I would be in a place where I belonged. My savings from the last five years could be put back into the farm. I could set up a quality retraining program with versatile horses. As I began training them, I would watch the horses grow, learn what their skills were. Not all horses were the same. While some had the powerful body and keen eye for jumping, others carried themselves in such a graceful way dressage would be perfect for them. But regardless of skill, a good horse would always work hard and aim to please.

Sighing, I turned my attention back to the game. Andrew ran into space, urging Sebastian to pass the ball to him. In a split-second, Sebastian glanced around to assess his position. His gaze paused ever so slightly on the two opposition players to Andrew's right. It may have appeared that Andrew was in the clear but if Sebastian passed the ball to him, one of the two players would intercept. Instead of passing, Sebastian hit the ball through a pack of players and followed it skilfully. He was so aware of the position of his team mates that as the opposition players descended on him, he did a sneaky backward pass to Doug, the back player. Doug struck the ball towards the goal mouth.

Andrew was not marking his opposition player and that player reached the ball first. He struck it towards the opposite goal. As the players charged to the other end of the field, I noticed Brutus throw in a couple of pig roots. I couldn't help but smile at Andrew's scowl.

The bell rang, indicating the end of the chukka and half time. As the riders made their way back, Andrew was swinging his mallet carelessly and knocked Brutus near his knee. Brutus tensed on impact. I clenched my teeth and imagined Brutus taking a sudden leap sideways and Andrew falling flat on his arse. That thought alone brought a smile to my face.

I handed the two horses I was holding to one of our game grooms. I preferred to take the ridden horses down to the truck so I could give them a quick once over.

The closer they got, the more I willed myself to stay silent.

One more season. One more season and I would be leaving Brisbane. I would be going home to the farm three hours north. I would be away from this life. And the rich snobs that formed a part of it.

Stay silent.

CHAPTER TWO

Sebastian

As we approached Frankie, Andrew was rambling on about meeting the ladies at half time. The quicker he removed himself from my vicinity the better. I dreaded each time his name came up on our team list. The man irritated me to no end. And the fact that he'd hit Brutus on the leg with his mallet and showed no concern or remorse made me dislike him even more.

He jumped off Brutus with exaggerated energy and shoved the reins at Frankie without even so much as a thank you. I caught Juan's eye and his scowl showed he felt the same.

Frankie took the reins off Doug who thanked her before she began walking back to the truck. After a few steps she stopped, bent over and ran her hand down Brutus's leg. She didn't miss a thing. Always watching. Always making sure the horses were OK. I'd even seen her approach grooms from other teams to converse with them about their horses if she had concerns. Sometimes she would offer advice about particular behaviours. I'd only ever seen one person take offence to her unsolicited advice. For her, no matter what, the horses came first.

Andrew nudged my leg. With raised eyebrows and a point of his chin in Frankie's direction, he said, "I wouldn't mind tapping that."

I clenched my reins and tensed so much I was surprised my horse didn't jolt out from beneath me.

Frankie stiffened and stood up. The curves that were evident when she had bent over disappeared beneath her polo shirt as she readjusted it. Red rose up her neck to her face. Without a glance backwards, she strode away.

I turned to him. "You–"

"You should go mingle," Juan interrupted in his Argentinian accent. He'd stopped me so it didn't turn heated. It's not something we would want the spectators or officials to see. And trust me, it would have become heated with the words I wanted to unload on him.

Andrew turned to the field and grinned before sauntering off. I dismounted and followed Frankie, passing Amanda on the way.

"Frankie," I called out. What was I going to say? It's not like it was my place to apologise for Andrew. She squared her shoulders and turned to me. Her hazel eyes were hard. By George, if looks could kill, my brain would have imploded.

"Is Brutus's leg OK?"

Her hard stare did not diminish with my question. "It's fine. Thanks."

I'd faced many a cold stare during my time at boarding

school but she outdid any of them. I shifted from foot to foot. "Lucky, the boot took most of the force."

"Lucky is not what I'd call it."

"No, I just meant–"

Frankie walked away.

"I'll take your horse," Amanda said, approaching from behind. "Go and get a drink with Doug and Juan."

I handed the reins over but didn't turn. I watched Frankie until she reached the truck fifteen metres away. After tying Brutus up, she rested her hand on his chest. Her posture relaxed. She patted him and said, "Sorry Brutus, it looks like we are surrounded by idiots today."

I'd encountered many men like Andrew, both at university and in my five years touring and playing polo. They were terrible brutes and their behaviour towards women was Neanderthal. Their actions and thoughts set equality back decades. I found it difficult to believe that some women liked that behaviour. My mother certainly wouldn't.

I didn't want to think of my mother. The Queen. The mere thought of her always put a dampener on my spirits. She was sure to call again soon to pressure me to return to my duties. To return to the country I was expected to rule. The country I hadn't lived in for fifteen years. No, I didn't want to think about my mother. There were better things to think about. I turned my attention back to Frankie.

CHAPTER THREE

Frankie

I FLICKED my finger up and down and Brutus nodded in agreement: we were surrounded by idiots. Sebastian chuckled from where I had left him. I ignored him. When I snuck a look in his direction he was walking away.

Amanda approached. "You know Sebastian was only trying to be nice."

I gave her the side-eye. "Nice?"

"Come on, Frankie, Sebastian's a good guy."

"Good for him."

"Don't act so haughty."

"I'm not."

I wasn't the one who was haughty. He was...from day one.

I looked up from where I was sitting at the desk as Sebastian and Juan walked into our office side by side. Amanda and I stood up to greet them. Juan walked over and gave us a wide smile. His handshake was friendly. Sebastian stood in the door-

way, stiff and awkward, clutching a wad of paper. He fit the polo part perfectly with his designer jeans and Ralph Lauren polo. I could go to Kmart and buy ten shirts for the price of just that one.

"I'm Amanda and this is Frankie. We are happy to have you with us this season."

Juan nodded. "We are happy to be here with you. We have never played a season in Australia before." His Argentinian accent was strong; his voice and pronunciation smooth. "I'm Juan and this is Sebastian."

Sebastian strode across the room and, without so much as a hello, he thrust the paperwork at us. "Non-disclosure agreements for you to sign."

I couldn't believe he was so rude. I snatched the paper from him and made a point of signing his stupid NDA without even reading it. When I was finished, I rammed it back into his hands, making sure my hazel eyes met his brown ones and held them. I wasn't going to be intimidated by him, his good looks or his royal title.

Amanda handed her two horses off, sighed and started unsaddling Brutus while I took off the bandages. We always took them off as soon as we could to avoid overheating the tendons. The more heat in tendon cells the more likely they are to be damaged or die. The methodical unwinding took my mind off the conversation. The warm, soft fleece brushed my fingers.

"How many times have we worked with Sebastian and Juan?" Amanda asked.

God, she wasn't going to give up.

"Most days over the past few months."

"Right. They've been at the stables with us just about every day for nearly four months. And have either of them ever been rude, apart from the NDA episode you like to remind me about?"

"No."

What was she getting at?

"And they've been respectful. Nice, even?"

I huffed. "Yes."

"Then why don't you give him a chance? Try being nice back?"

"I am nice."

"Is that what you call it?"

"That's not fair. I'm usually nice. I just didn't want to deal with him after what Andrew said." I explained to her what happened.

"Don't you think maybe Sebastian was trying to make sure you were OK but didn't want to make you feel uncomfortable?"

I hadn't thought of that.

"Sebastian notices things, Frankie. He's not like some other players here. He doesn't act nice. He *is* nice. Juan, too."

"Yeah. OK."

I handed Brutus over to one of the game grooms to cool down and hose. I watched him walk away. He was putting full weight on his leg and his head wasn't bobbing like it did when he was in pain.

Amanda busied herself hanging hay nets. I thought the conversation was over until she said, "I'm sure Sebastian likes you."

How was I even supposed to respond to that? I'd fallen for

nice before. And I wasn't about to do it again. I was sick of rich guys thinking they could get what they want just by flashing a smile. Nice or not nice. Prince or no prince.

I grabbed the gear and walked away.

CHAPTER FOUR

Sebastian

I WATCHED, bemused, as the spectator's divot stomped their way around the field. Men laughed with gusto, trying to beat each other to the next piece of upturned turf. Ladies in their high heels pushed the grass and dirt back into place, smoothing out the surface. I was sure they'd be barefoot by the end of the day. When you'd played as many tournaments as we had, you knew the patterns. Polo involved a lot of standing for spectators, even if they were in a VIP marquee. A small group of ladies were clinging to each other, giggling between sips of champagne and teetering on their heels as they joined in the tradition. Unsurprisingly, Andrew beelined towards this group.

I turned my attention to some children nearby who were having a grand time jumping up and down on the churned grass. One small blonde girl, maybe aged seven, moved her eyes from one end of the field to the other. She bit her lip as she turned her attention to the boys next to her.

I went and stood beside her. "It's big, isn't it?"

"Yes. The horses must get tired running up and down all the time."

"Yes, they do. That's why every time the bell rings we change horses."

Her big blue eyes regarded me. "But don't you get tired too?"

"I sure do. Although, the horses do most of the work. That's why they deserve a rest."

She watched the people as they attacked the divots. "Why does everyone stomp the ground?"

"Have you ever seen a horse's hoof up close?"

She shook her head. I looked at the mounting area. Frankie had returned with Ruby. "Would you like to meet one?"

I don't know what was wider, her eyes or her grin. She nodded.

We walked over to the mounting area at the edge of the field. Spectators were standing by, conversing and watching the horses. I made a beeline for Frankie and Ruby. "This is Frankie. She looks after our horses. And this is Ruby."

The girl leant her head backwards, staring up at Ruby's face. Ruby lowered her head and sniffed at the girl, who giggled.

"If you like, you can give Ruby a rub on her nose. Reach your hand out slowly. It's always important not to move fast when saying hello to an animal."

She reached out and touched Ruby. The touch became a gentle pat.

"She's so soft," the girl whispered.

"Now, remember we were talking about the stomping?"

She nodded.

"Frankie, can you show...what's your name, sweetie?"

"Lily."

"Can you please show Lily Ruby's hoof?"

Frankie bent and squeezed Ruby's chestnut on the front leg closest to Lily. Ruby lifted her foot and Frankie caught it.

"See how big her hoof is?" I put my hand against the hoof so Lily could compare the size. "And see the edges around the hoof?" I ran my finger around the outside so Lily could see what I was talking about. "Now, let's go and look at the field." I stood up. "Thanks, Frankie, for showing us."

Frankie let Ruby's leg go.

"And thank you, Ruby," Lily said. She didn't follow.

"You can give her a hug goodbye," Frankie said.

Lily considered and then wrapped her small arms around Ruby's leg. When she was finished, I led her back to the field and knelt down.

"So just imagine Ruby is running really fast and her hooves are digging into the ground. Sometimes she turns quickly."

Lily nodded. I picked up a clump of grass.

"This is what happens to the field. It gets churned up. So, all of these people are now stomping these bits of grass and dirt back into place."

Lily and I watched the crowd. Some of them had nearly made it to the other end of the field. The boys she had been with earlier were chasing each other around the goals. I turned my attention back to Lily.

"Pushing them back in means Ruby and the other horses are less likely to twist or fall and hurt themselves."

"Oh, that's good," Lily said, glancing back at Ruby. I followed her gaze. Ruby and Frankie were watching us.

The bell sounded and the spectators made their way off the field. Lily threw her arms around my neck, said a quick thank you, and ran off.

I smiled. This was the type of thing I'd miss if I returned to Oleander, the freedom to speak to whoever I wanted, whenever I wanted. Instead, I'd have bodyguards close by and cameras following my every move. I had bodyguards here with me, at my family's insistence, but they kept their distance. Only those close to me knew they existed. Actually, only those close knew that I was the Crown Prince of Oleander. I liked it that way. I shook my head. I didn't want to think about Oleander or returning there any time soon.

Before Lily crossed the barrier, she turned and gave me a wave. I returned it and walked back to a smiling Frankie. When she smiled her whole face lit up, even her hazel eyes. Her face hardened when she realised my attention was on her.

I didn't know what I'd done. We'd spent a lot of time together over the past few months, but she always kept me at arm's length. I didn't take offence to it. It didn't make me feel uncomfortable; she was always friendly and helpful. Some people just liked to keep their inner circle small. I was one of them, but I hoped she'd open up more over time. I found her energy drew me in and she intrigued me.

As I approached, I noticed Doug was with her, not Andrew. Amanda must have moved him to the other groom after what had happened. As soon as I reached the mounting area, Frankie shoved Ruby's reins at me.

"I hope she's fast enough for you."

Turning her back on me, she went to Doug's side and checked his horse's girth. Laughter between them erupted as she helped him mount. She was such a contradiction. Happy and relaxed around Doug, and as cold and dark as the winter solstice with me.

I mounted and caressed the leather reins with my fingers. The familiarity of the leather brushing against my calloused hands grounded me. It would horrify my mother that my hands were rough like a true worker's. A royal's hands, in her view, should be soft and supple for all the hand shaking.

I rode out to join Juan. I had only one thought on my mind, apart from the way Frankie's face lit up when she laughed, and that was that I couldn't play the next chukka closely with Andrew. Not without risking a mallet to his head.

"Can we swap positions please?"

Juan's hefty eyebrows rose. With a smile, he said, "*You* want to play defence?"

"For the sake of continuing to be a part of this team, yes."

I glared in Andrew's direction.

"Ah, yes, anyone would think *he* was in line to ascend the throne the way he acts."

"You know I would gladly give up the throne."

"But not to someone like him."

"No. As much as I want to get away from that life, I would never subject the people of Oleander to the likes of him." I tried to keep my face passive but the tone of my voice said it all. It was another reason why I would not make a good king. I couldn't hold my emotions back. My dislike of people or situations would always show too clearly.

"Spoken like a true nobleman." He laughed as he rode off towards Andrew.

CHAPTER FIVE

Frankie

Ruby and I cantered around the field, leading two other horses. With over 40 horses at our polo stables, exercising looked like this most days, unless we were doing individual training with them. With the green grass below us and the blue sky above, it was a perfect setting. At the end of the field where we were exercising, the trees grew thick creating a windbreak. To our left were fenced paddocks and on our right the view of hills and bushland stretched far into the distance. Riding here was a privilege.

As we turned and headed back to the other end, I saw Juan and Sebastian watching us. Ugh, as if a weekend with Sebastian wasn't enough. Couldn't they just have a day off? I took a deep breath and prepared myself mentally. Juan stepped forward when I was close.

"I'd like to work on turns with the younger horses this morning," Juan said.

"In the sand arena?" It would be better for them on the

sand surface, less pressure on their muscles and joints. I ignored the smile that crept onto Sebastian's face.

"Yes, mama, in the sand arena. Does mama want to make sure I'm training them right too?" Juan laughed as he tugged at my leg.

"Maybe I should. I don't need you teaching them any fancy Argentinian Tango steps."

"Come, I'll show you how real men dance."

Sebastian piped up. "What are you saying? Only Argentinian men can dance?"

"No, I'm saying only Argentinian men are real men."

Laughter escaped my lips. Suffer in ya jocks, Sebastian.

Sebastian ran his hand through this sandy brown hair messing it up. It didn't take much effort to mess up with how long it had grown throughout the season. Even with messy hair he looked stylish. And that just complimented his royal good looks with his wide jaw and perfectly symmetrical face. Argh, was being perfect a prerequisite to being royal? I rolled my eyes, reminding myself he wasn't *that* perfect. The way he insisted we all sign non-disclosure agreements when he arrived raised my hackles. It wasn't the fact that we needed to sign them. That I could understand. It was the way he tossed them to us and his dismissive attitude.

Juan squeezed my calf drawing my attention back to him. "We'll see if those nice legs of yours can keep up."

"I can keep up with you any day."

Juan's grin widened. He was so good natured I couldn't help but laugh with him. I dismounted and faced him. I wouldn't let him and his Argentinian dance skills intimidate me.

"Ah, what a shame. Today isn't the day for me. Today, I need you to dance with Sebastian."

"What?" The laughter died in my throat. There was no way I was dancing with Sebastian, even if it was just as a joke on a polo field.

"Oooh, are you worried you can't keep up with a prince?"

Keep up with him? If I were to dance with him, which I would not, he would have trouble keeping up with me.

"I'm not dancing with Sebastian."

"Come now, it's easy." Juan grabbed me around the waist and pulled me into a close embrace. "Now, imagine it is Sebastian you are dancing with," he whispered in my ear. Amanda's voice echoed after his: *I'm sure Sebastian likes you.*

The thought of Sebastian being as close to me as Juan was, unsettled me. I imagined his strong arms holding me. Our hearts beating together. My head resting on his shoulder, his well-toned shoulder. My pulse increased and I blushed at the thought. I pulled away.

"I'm not dancing with Sebastian."

"Ah, but you'd dance with me."

"Yes...well...but–"

Sebastian cleared his throat. "I need you to run drills with me."

"Dancing on horseback." Juan laughed.

Drills. Not dance. What an idiot.

Juan continued to guffaw. He squeezed my shoulders and kissed my cheek. "Francesca darling, the look on your face."

My face reddened.

"Rack off." I pulled on Ruby's reins and walked away with her and the other horses trailing.

"Oh boy, I must have hit a raw nerve," Juan called after me.

"Shut up," Sebastian said, mirroring my sentiments.

Raw nerve alright. After the conversation with Amanda yesterday I would prefer to stay away from Sebastian. I didn't need a prince to think I could be a jewel in his crown. I sped up. Sebastian's footsteps were steady and determined behind me.

"How's Brutus this morning?"

"Fine."

Sebastian was beside me.

"Is he sore from that hit from Andrew?"

"No."

I slowed my pace in resignation.

"Does he have any swelling?"

"No."

As I took the horses to the tack up area Sebastian stopped at Brutus's yard.

I sighed. "I put him in there overnight so I could check on him first thing this morning. I Tuff Rocked the affected area to help with any swelling or soreness. There is no swelling where he was hit. I've run my hand up and down the limb, there is no heat there. And he doesn't move away from my touch."

I turned to face him. Sebastian was no longer at the gate; he was inside the yard with Brutus. What? Didn't he think I could diagnose or treat an injury? I may not be a royal veterinarian but I knew about horses. I'd treated some bad injuries on the farm. Those horses never had a complaint.

I dropped Ruby's lead rope and stormed over. My fists

clenched as anger blurred my vision. "I know how to treat injuries. I've–"

Sebastian wasn't checking Brutus's leg or doing any sort of assessment. Instead Brutus's head was resting in Sebastian's arms while Sebastian patted him with long, loving strokes. He was talking quietly to him.

I stood there like an idiot, as if I'd walked in on an intimate moment between father and son. I wanted to turn around and pretend I hadn't just stormed over. But I couldn't stop watching them. That touch, the way Brutus responded with a breath that quivered his lips, his eyes drooping, was a perfect example of love between man and horse.

Sebastian gave a final stroke and moved away from Brutus. When he glanced at me and smiled, I thought my heart might fly out of my chest. I stepped backwards.

"I was telling Brutus that he's a good boy. And that next time if...if...Andrew hit him, I give him full permission to drop him on his arse."

I nodded, taking another step backwards.

"I'm not sure Brutus has it in him, though."

"No, he doesn't."

Sebastian shouldn't know that. Why did Sebastian know that? Amanda's words echoed in my mind. *Sebastian notices things, Frankie.* I went back to Ruby and the other horses. "I'll take these to the paddock. Who do you want me to bring back?"

Sebastian came and stood beside me. "Any four that are still in training. I'll come with you. It will be easier for me to hold them while you drive the quad."

My stomach did a small lurch, like it did when I was about to start a barrel race. I shook my head and the feeling dissipated. Why was he offering to help? Didn't he have people waiting on him back home, ready to attend to his every need? Isn't that what he expected me to do?

"It's OK. I can go on my own. That's what I'm here for."

"It will be safer with two of us. Four will be a handful for you to bring back on your own."

"OK."

I couldn't say no to him. It was a good idea. My discomfort, or whatever it was that made my body react to his closeness, would just have to disappear.

"You need to lead Ruby on her own on the left. She doesn't like being led with other horses." Some horses were followers, others were leaders. All of them had their own preferences.

We hopped on the quad and led the three horses back to the paddock. I was acutely aware of how close Sebastian was sitting behind me. The warmth of his legs seeped through my jeans. When I took a corner too fast his hand would rest against my waist so he could steady himself. The lurch in my stomach happened each time. I slowed down so he didn't need to touch me.

When we arrived back Sebastian handed two horses to me to start tacking up while he put the other two in a yard.

"What drills are we going to do?" I asked.

"These two have worked alone so far. They've had a rider on their back, they've felt how a rider moves in a game and they've had a mallet flying past their heads to get them desensitised."

I nodded. I'd done a lot of that work myself. We'd galloped for miles every week.

"They've exercised together so they're accustomed to

being close to other horses. Now we need to see how they do when there is intention involved. They need to learn to play together," he said.

I knew all of this. After nearly five years at the polo stables, I'd been involved with training the new horses. I usually worked on flatwork and fitness. A lot of people underestimate the importance of flatwork and teaching basic dressage. It's the foundation for all riding, whether it be in a jumping arena or on the polo field. It teaches a horse balance, how to carry themselves, and responsiveness.

It was time they started to learn the different pressures involved with playing. Moving intentionally after a ball while the other horses were doing the same. The bumps, the speed, the sharp turns, all with other horses, not just on their own. Some horses would get frightened if another horse galloped up behind them. They needed to be desensitised to that. Some off the track thoroughbreds forgot where they were, and if a horse galloped up behind them, they took off like they were in a race. They needed to learn to remember they weren't race horses anymore.

"You already know all of this. Sorry," Sebastian said.

"That's OK. Sometimes it's easier to start at the beginning when explaining."

"You'd be surprised at how many people get upset when you try to gauge their knowledge and experience."

"Oh, I know. Some polo players don't understand I'm just doing what's best for the horses when I ask them questions."

"I can imagine."

I'm sure we both thought of the same person as we smiled at each other.

We headed out to the field with balls and mallets and

started to play. It wasn't fast or tidy but the horses were comfortable and learning. We sped up as the horses grew confident.

Sebastian's phone sounded, indicating the end of fifteen minutes, and we swapped the horses. I liked the way Sebastian trained. He was quiet and patient with the horses. He told a horse when it was doing the right thing. And if it wasn't, he didn't reprimand, he just took it as a learning experience and helped the horse get to where he wanted it to be.

As we headed back to the office he said, "The horses are lucky to have you."

Where had that come from?

"For someone who isn't technically trained you have a good swing plane. That helps your horse remain balanced."

I peered at him sideways. "Thanks. Juan taught me how to rotate my shoulder and extend my mallet back, rather than rotate my body."

He nodded and smiled. "A good teacher and a good student. Can I give you one other tip?"

I nodded.

"Try not to grip the mallet like you're strangling someone. If you hold it in your fingers rather than your palm the mallet becomes an extension of your arm directly in line with your shoulder."

I nodded. I'd try it later when he wasn't around.

"Are you coming to the fundraiser ball at the casino tonight?" he asked, glancing over at me.

"I'd rather not. But Amanda pulled rank and said I need to go seeing I'm her assistant manager."

He smiled. "Great. Juan and I are heading off now. That will give you plenty of time to get ready."

"Are you saying I need a lot of time to get ready?" He had some nerve.

"That's not what I said. I just know females take a long time."

"Really?"

"Well, my mother usually does."

"Maybe a queen has the luxury of taking all day to get ready. The rest of us mere mortals can manage in much less time." I stared him down, my teeth grinding.

"I didn't–"

"Don't bother. I know exactly what you meant. I hope I can make myself at least half decent to be welcomed in your presence. *Prince.*"

Arrogant arse.

I walked away.

"ISN'T it nice to get dressed up for a change?" Amanda asked, entering my bathroom and twirling around.

"Yes." I smiled at her. Her black dress flared out as she spun. "It feels weird though. I haven't worn heels in ages. I hope I can walk."

I finished putting on my lipstick and turned to her. She let out a low whistle.

"Trust me girl, no one is going to care how you walk when you look like that."

"Not bad for a forty-dollar second hand dress."

The dark red, short-sleeved dress was fitted and showed just enough cleavage that I was able to wear a bra. Having a D cup, I didn't feel comfortable going braless. I had my Italian heritage to thank for having ample breasts. There was a long slit that went to mid-thigh.

"Sebastian will be knocked off his feet."

"I don't really care if Sebastian is knocked off his feet. Or anyone else for that matter."

"Come on, you need someone to dance with."

I gave her a sidelong glance. "Have you been speaking to Juan?"

"No. Why?"

"Doesn't matter."

I walked out of the bathroom.

She stalked me down the corridor in her black dress like she was a panther.

"Why would I want to speak to Juan?"

"No reason."

"If there was no reason, why did you ask?"

"It was just a question."

"I mentioned Sebastian, and then dancing and then you asked if I'd spoken to Juan. Why?"

She was like an annoying little sister. She would keep badgering me until I told her something. Anything. I needed it to be at least part truth or else she would pick up on the lie. I wasn't a very good liar. I didn't do it often enough.

"Juan was just talking about doing the tango."

"With you?"

"Yes."

Her eyes narrowed and I could see her bite the inside of her cheek. Shit.

"What's that got to do with Sebastian?" she said.

Shit.

"Nothing. Come on, let's go. Our cab's here."

We sat in silence as the cab pulled out of our driveway until she asked, "Do you like Sebastian?"

"Hell no. He's rich. He's a snob. And he's arrogant."

"He's not arrogant."

I didn't bother arguing. She wasn't going to listen. I hoped she didn't think my silence meant I agreed.

"And he's a prince," I blurted out.

"So?"

"So, we come from two totally different worlds. His arrogant arse belongs in a castle, my home is on the farm."

"Mm." She turned her head away but not before I saw her mischievous smile. She drummed her fingers on her leg. I huffed and glared out the other window watching as the trees thinned out and the outskirts of suburbia appeared. Street lights streamed past and I wished the glow was from the moon and stars at home instead. There was no such thing as light pollution on the farm. The stars and moon shone so bright you could ride at night.

Amanda turned back to me. "You know just because he's rich it doesn't mean he's a bad person."

"Yeah, well, rich and I don't go well together. I prefer the simpler things in life."

"You can't judge every rich person based on Steve-I've-Got -So Much-Money-I- Can Have-Who-I-Want-And-More-Than-One-At-A-Time-If-I-So-Please."

I knew I shouldn't put everyone in the same boat as Steve. That man knew how to play the game. And he would have kept on playing too, if he hadn't been caught.

CHAPTER SIX

Sebastian

"Would you stop looking at the door?" Juan said, taking a sip of his red wine.

"I'm not."

"Really? Then why does your head turn every time the door opens?"

"It doesn't."

I grabbed at my bow tie and adjusted it. The door opened again but I kept my eyes on my whiskey. I made a point to look around the large function room. Round chandeliers hung from the ceiling. They matched the sphere lights on long stems that sat on each of the tables. The chair covers and tablecloths were cream satin. They reflected the warmth from the lighting.

"Who are you waiting for anyway?" Andrew asked from across the table. Just the sight of his slicked back blonde hair and smarmy grin irritated me. His slightly crooked nose could have been considered rugged and attractive, if it didn't belong to him. And that white suit was as pretentious as he was. How the hell we got stuck with him I don't know. He could have sat at half a dozen other tables, where he knew people, but no, he had to be seated with us. It was probably a strategic business move by Amanda. Keeping Andrew on side could bring in extra sponsorship.

I fiddled with my bow tie again.

"Stop playing with that thing," Juan said, giving me a friendly nudge.

"I bet your nanny told you that a lot," Andrew said, laughing at his own joke.

I scowled. How was I going to sit there all night with him and not say something I'd regret?

"It feels like it's strangling me," I said to Juan.

"I thought you'd be used to wearing one, being royalty and all." Juan's voice was quiet so no one else on the table could hear. I was sure Andrew would have something extra obnoxious to say if he'd heard.

It was true. I had worn a bow tie to special events from an early age. Maybe it was just that correlation that made me feel like I couldn't breathe. Just because I was born into that life it didn't mean it was the life for me. The thought of living it was suffocating.

"Hot damn," Andrew exclaimed from across the table.

I followed his line of sight. Frankie and Amanda stood in the doorway. When Amanda spotted us, she waved and pulled on Frankie's arm. Blood rushed in my ears when I took in every inch of Frankie. She was stunning. Beautiful. Her red dress hugged her body in all the right places. The cut accentuated her breasts. Did noticing them make me sexist like Andrew? Even the thought that I could be compared to him didn't force my eyes away. Frankie's brown hair, normally tied in a pony tail fell around her shoulders. Her full lips were coated in dark red lipstick that matched her dress.

"Fuck me. I know who I'm going home with tonight," Andrew said, from across the table.

I stood up and glared at him. What I wanted to do was go over there, haul him out of his chair and punch him so hard he wouldn't be able to speak.

"What, you want her as a princely conquest?" Andrew sneered at me.

"Bas," Juan cautioned.

"If you so much as utter one more crude thing tonight, I will punch your lights out. You are to do nothing but treat those two ladies with respect."

What was wrong with me? Threatening someone was a very unroyal thing to do. Andrew's stared at me with wide eyes. Doug, seated beside him, smiled. I didn't turn to Juan to see his reaction.

The room disappeared in my wake as I made my way to Frankie and Amanda. The low music died in my ears. The people talking at the tables vanished. All I could concentrate on was Frankie.

When I reached them, I gave them both a kiss on the cheek. "Amanda, you look beautiful."

"Thank you," she said, holding onto my forearm lightly.

My eyes rested on Frankie. Those red lips and striking hazel eyes had me mesmerised. She had a scar on her left arm that stretched from her bicep to tricep. I'd noticed it before but as she was in a short-sleeved dress today, it stood out. What had caused it? I was sure it must have been horse related. It seemed like everything she did was horse related.

Like a fourteen-year-old boy looking at his crush, my brain froze.

"And how do I look? Seeing as I didn't have all day to get ready, I hope I look *alright*." The hardness in Frankie's voice brought me back to reality.

"You look more than alright."

She nodded and walked away. Her body was made for that dress. And the way that slit opened up to reveal her toned legs could keep my attention all night. It wasn't just my attention she captured. As she weaved her way through the tables some people stopped talking to watch her.

"If you stick your tongue back in your mouth, perhaps you can tell me what that was all about?" Amanda said, turning to me.

"Nothing."

"Really? Nothing? Nothing to do with you being arrogant?"

"I'm not arrogant." My heart dropped. "Does Frankie think I'm arrogant?"

"I'm not sure what Frankie thinks, anymore."

By the time we reached the table Juan had changed the place cards around so Amanda was on his left and Frankie on his right, with me on her other side. Thankfully Doug still filled the chair next to me.

"Would the lovely ladies like a cocktail?" Andrew asked.

Amanda picked up the drink menu. "They're not serving cocktails."

"For you, anything is possible. How about some Cock Sucking Cowboys?"

I put my glass down on the table and turned to Andrew. What was he playing at?

"Sure, as long as you're going to have one, too," Amanda said, smirking at him.

"I'd rather a cowgirl, like Frankie here."

Frankie shifted in her seat beside me. I was about to stand until Doug kicked me in the shin.

"I'll stick with champagne," she said.

"Suit yourself."

Andrew got up and went to a nearby table. Frankie sat back and sipped on her champagne. A faint scent of roses drifted to me as she tossed her hair. Meanwhile, Amanda turned in her seat, her lips twitching like she was suppressing a smile.

"Juan, I hear you are going to dance the tango with Frankie tonight."

Frankie took a sharp breath in and stiffened beside me. She drowned the remainder of her champagne before placing her glass on the table. Doug reached over for her glass to refill it. She smiled at him. I may as well have not even been at the table.

"No. No, not me," Juan said. "Frankie is going to dance with Sebastian."

Frankie downed her second glass.

"Oh, she is, is she?"

"No, she is not," Frankie said, sitting forward and indicating to Doug for another refill.

"I'm sure that's what we spoke about today," Juan smiled at her. Her reaction was like bait to him.

"If I recall correctly, you were saying to me that you would show me how real men dance. You. Not him." She finished her drink in one gulp. Pink was rising in her cheeks.

"Did someone say dance? I'd love to have the first dance

with you, Frankie," Andrew said resting his hand on her shoulder.

Frankie smiled at Juan before she answered. "Sure, I'd love that too."

Had the champagne gone to her head? As the entrée came to the table, I poured a glass of water for each of us. I turned my attention to the plate of smoked kangaroo, beetroot and goat cheese salad. The colours on the plate were bold but the plating itself was delicate, with the kangaroo sliced so thinly it was like ribbon.

We sat through the auction where Andrew bidded big, driving up the prices on holidays, signed jerseys with team photos, and jewellery, but never actually winning anything. I considered whether he lost on purpose.

We had a presentation from the president of Riding for the Disabled. It was heart-warming to watch the videos of the children and adults riding. The smiles on their faces were infectious.

After that we were invited up to the donation table. I chose for my ten-thousand-dollar donation to remain anonymous. When I got back to the table Andrew was in my seat. His hand was on Frankie's elbow. My stomach tightened. When he spotted me, he raised his eyebrows. I settled into his chair.

"I donated two thousand dollars. The lady was so happy. She said it would feed one of their horses for a year."

Frankie smiled at him. Was that smile genuine?

"The music's starting. Let's go," he said, standing up and reaching for her hand.

Frankie glanced at Amanda who gave a tiny shrug.

"Come on, you promised the first dance to me."

She stood up. I stiffened as he rested his hand on the small of her back. I could almost feel his smirk smack me in the face. As soon as they reached the dance floor, he pulled her in close. She rested her hands on his chest.

"Sebastian..."

I didn't register anything but my name. My breathing was harsh. What the hell was wrong with me? Frankie could dance with whoever she wanted to. But with him? She knew what he was like.

Andrew's hand drifted down from its resting spot on her waist. With every centimetre my body clenched a bit more. He said something to her. Frankie took hold of his neck, pulled his head towards her and spoke into his ear. Whatever she said had an instant effect. His hand withdrew. She let go of him and pushed him away. The tension in my muscles dissipated.

That's the Frankie I knew.

CHAPTER SEVEN

Frankie

I watched Andrew walk away, fast. Threatening to cut off someone's testicles will have that effect. If that didn't give him a clear message, I'm sure kicking him between the legs would.

I turned towards our table and walked straight into Sebastian. My stomach did that lurch as he took a step backwards and held out his hand to me. I stared at it and then back at his face.

"May I have this dance?"

I took his hand. There wasn't really any other option. He gathered me in his arms and we moved around the dance floor. The live band played an alluring melody, one that was sultry and managed to reach right into my centre. I relaxed into Sebastian's embrace, knowing I didn't have to worry about wandering hands. When he bent his head to mine, his warm breath brushing against my ear, tingles spread across my skin.

"What did you say to Andrew?"

"I asked him if he had ever seen a horse castrated. Then I offered to demonstrate on him if he touched me again."

His chuckle made me feel content. What was wrong with me? This was Sebastian, a man I didn't particularly like. The man who was a prince and thought he was above everyone else. The song ended and we lingered for another.

Sebastian pulled me in closer for the slow dance. Heat spread through me at his closeness, and I rested my head against his shoulder. God, he smelled good: earthy and sensual. His cheek moved against my hair giving me the impression he was smiling. I pulled away to look up into his face. My breath hitched as I gazed into his soulful brown eyes. My lips were millimetres from his and I could feel his breath whisper against them. I licked my lips at the hint of whiskey shared between us, trying to savour it.

We moved as if one and I was lost in him. It dawned on me that music no longer filled the air and I pulled away. My hands, which a moment ago had been holding him, felt empty. I smoothed my dress down to keep them busy. His eyes followed their movement and I felt them every inch of the way. What if they were his hands and not his eyes? I shivered at the thought.

I sucked in my breath and made my way back to the table with Sebastian following. Andrew was nowhere to be seen. I breathed a sigh of relief; I didn't want to put up with any snide comments.

"Juan is going to show us his poker skills at the casino," Amanda said.

"He tells us he'll be able to beat anyone here," Doug added, chuckling like he didn't believe him.

"Are those poker skills just like your dance skills? All talk?" I teased.

Juan put his hand over his heart. "Oh Francesca, your words pain me. Shall we dance now?"

What had I gotten myself into? "Is this a ploy to distract me from poker?"

"Ah, I see. Sebastian is the only one you will dance with."

"I danced with Andrew, too."

"Yes, but we all saw how you scared him away. We know who you wanted to dance with all along."

Sebastian shifted in his seat. I cut him off before he could say anything about dancing with me so I wasn't stranded alone on the dance floor.

"Are we going to play poker or what?" I asked.

"You play poker?" Juan asked, his eyes wide.

"Strip poker," Amanda said, laughing across the table. Doug joined in.

"I never lost a game. The stakes were too high."

That made Doug laugh even more. I didn't look at Sebastian for his reaction. I doubt he would have played a game of strip poker in his life, being a prince and all.

Doug had trouble speaking through his laughter. "The last time I played strip poker I lost so bad I had to do a nudie run down the street."

I could just picture it. Doug with his vibrant red hair and pale body contrasted against the dark night and black tar road. His bouncing balls–

"Stop thinking about it," Sebastian whispered in my ear.

"I wasn't." Heat crept up my cheeks.

"Really? Why did you have that funny look in your eyes?"

"I didn't."

Sebastian notices things, Frankie.

"Come on, let's go," Amanda said.

When we hit the poker table, Juan was good. I lasted longer that Amanda and Doug and bowed out after a few games, leaving Juan at the table with other players. He had no tell that I could see. He didn't tap his cards or play with his chips depending on what type of hand he had. His posture never changed. He was his usual happy self regardless of what hand he was dealt.

"You don't play?" I asked Sebastian who was standing beside me. Amanda and Doug were at the bar.

"No point. I'm not very good at it."

"No strip poker for you?" It was a light hearted dig. I wanted to see his reaction.

My mind wandered to what he would look like butt naked in front of me and it was totally different to how I saw Doug. Amanda would be impressed. I blushed.

He didn't bite. "Not much fun in an all-male boarding school."

"I suppose. What do you do for fun in an all-male boarding school?"

"Play polo. Spend time with the horses."

"Is that it? Surely you snuck out to meet girls?"

"Sometimes. It didn't interest me much though."

"What sort of guy isn't interested in meeting girls?" Maybe Sebastian required too many non-disclosure agreements and the girls told him to stick it. I sure would have liked to stick his NDA somewhere. I felt like it was always hanging over our heads, something he used to look down on us.

He shrugged.

"Oh, I get it, a prince would only be interested in royalty."

It came out harsher than I meant it to. Sebastian took a step away and peered down at me. His mouth was tight.

"There are more important things than just royalty. I'd prefer to be with someone I genuinely like. Someone who shares the same interests and has the same dreams."

As Amanda and Doug approached Sebastian strode towards them, grabbed his drink and kept going.

"Did you two have a lovers' tiff?" Amanda asked. God, she was never going to let this go.

Juan finished his hand, collected his chips and stood beside me. "No, she questioned his integrity." He must have overheard.

"I did no such thing."

"Yes, you did. All you can see is his royal title. But you don't see him as the man he is."

What was he talking about? I knew Sebastian was a man. The way he had held me on the dance floor left no doubt. Juan peered at me like he was measuring me up, while his mouth worked from side to side. Then he nodded to himself.

"Oh Francesca, all his life he has tried to be more than his title. Do you see him flaunting it around? Do you see him introducing himself as a prince? He's a good man. He sees people as they are and treats them accordingly."

But he always acted superior. Or was I imagining it so I could classify him as another snobby rich person? I tried to think back and couldn't come up with any firm examples other than the NDA episode. Had I misjudged him?

CHAPTER EIGHT

Frankie

IT WAS a relief not to have Andrew on our team this week. At least I didn't have to worry about bending over in front of him or him getting too handsy. While Juan gave the team talk, I stood next to Amanda. There was a spot next to Sebastian but I avoided that like I had evaded him through the week.

I didn't know how to behave around him. What Juan had said about him being a good person made me feel bad. It was true. He was nice to us and kind to the horses.

I caught myself looking at him standing beside Juan as he talked about tactics. I couldn't deny he was good looking, with his hair a touch too long so it curled at his collar. And those eyes. I remembered how they had captured me on the dance floor. When I focused, I saw Sebastian watching me. He smiled and my only response was to blush. I averted my gaze to my feet and watched my toe dig a hole in the grass.

Amanda tugged at my arm. "Time to go."

I followed her to the truck and started tacking up Ruby.

"Were you even listening to Juan?" Amanda asked.

"What?"

"Juan wants to put the younger horses in first. The first team we're playing is less experienced than our normal opponents. They haven't been together long. And we have two five-goal players and their highest is a three-goal."

"Oh, OK."

That made sense. It would be good for our younger ones to have a run in a slower game. I tacked the horses up and led them up for the riders to mount. I gave Sebastian his horse first.

"Thank you, Frankie."

I nodded and handed him his mallet. He held it perfectly. He sat perfectly. He moved his horse off perfectly. I sighed. I guess when you were a royal you had time to be perfect.

I handed the other horse to another rider and turned to take the next two from Amanda. Standing there, I watched the game. It was a slower game than last week. Juan was in position three: his preferred position. It was the best suited to him as the player with the most experience. He and Sebastian often swapped between two and three. Their style and practical thinking were similar. They were both mid-ranked players and had played together for a long time.

Our number four was clearing his man to the edge of the field out of the play. Juan hit the ball softly so it travelled slowly. Sebastian recognised the play and moved towards the goal, outrunning his mark and always remaining ahead of him. He had such skill on the horse he made everything look easy. Juan followed the ball and hit it again for Sebastian to collect. The goal was free and he scored.

Sebastian gave Toro a big pat and I lip-read the words,

"Good boy."

I hadn't known much about polo when I started. I soon became impressed with the players – horses and humans alike. The horses put themselves into the game with their whole body, listening to their rider at all times, and doing whatever was asked of them. The humans weren't much different. They watched and listened, always thinking ahead, always aware of what was needed. Thinking quick, moving quick. That's what made Juan and Sebastian five-goal players. It was the way they played, their team work and their knowledge of the game.

The bell sounded signalling the end of the chukka. I held Sebastian's new horse in position while he shuffled across from Toro. The breaks between chukkas were so short it was the easiest way to go. I handed Toro off to Amanda and helped the other rider.

"Can I have some water please?" Sebastian asked.

I clenched my teeth. That damn posh voice annoyed me. Never mind that it was actually my job and I should have offered before he had to ask. I handed a bottle to the other player before giving Sebastian his.

The bell sounded and I took the bottles from the players. Sebastian held eye contact with me and I felt that stupid lurch. I tore my eyes away and turned my back on him. Amanda was there waiting with the next two horses giving me a funny look.

There was only one other time I hadn't been able to read her expression.

I walked back to the field with two horses for the players after half time. I was thinking about Steve. We'd spent the night together and that morning he told me how he was looking forward to meeting my family. He had asked me to arrange a weekend away at the farm. I was thrilled. Steve knew how important my family was to me. I was so excited I'd called my parents on the way to the game.

Thinking about him made me smile, like a giddy teenager. At twenty-one I'd thought I'd met the man of my dreams.

When I looked up, I saw Amanda and another groom approach me. Amanda had a strange look on her face – pain, disbelief, anger, I couldn't describe it. The groom took the horses and Amanda took my arm.

"I need to tell you something." Her voice was shaking.

"OK." I didn't know how else to respond.

She looked back towards the crowd. "Steve has a guest."

My brow furrowed. What could be the problem with that?

"His guest is his fiancé."

I stared at her dumbly.

"His what?"

"Fiancé."

I shook her hand free and marched up to the edge of the crowd where Steve was standing...with a bubbly blonde.

"Oh, I know why Steve loves polo so much now. The game is just to die for. Oh, and the atmosphere, it's just wonderful."

As she gushed on, Steve stood there with his hand on her waist smiling down at her. I couldn't draw my eyes away from his hand, the way they stood close together, the way she looked up at him with adoration. I broke into a sweat as nausea threatened to overtake me.

He spotted me and his mouth dropped open. "Frankie," he said, his voice strangled.

Miss Bubbly looked at me. She stepped away from Steve and came towards me.

"You must be the famous Frankie. Steve has told me so much about you."

Not nearly enough, it appeared. Not how he loved me as surely as the tide returns to the shore. Not how he bedded me and declared he had never felt so satisfied with life.

"I can't thank you enough for helping him improve his game. I've been envious of the time he's been spending with you." She embraced me like we were long lost friends. I stood stiffly. "He's hardly had any time to help with the wedding plans. I just had to come and see what polo was all about." As she spoke, I measured up Steve. He turned an interesting colour of green. He didn't attempt to intervene, to save me from embarrassment as others who knew of our relationship turned away.

Miss Bubbly pulled away and gave me a bright smile. She turned to Steve and he appeared by her side.

"I hope you enjoy your day," I said, smiling at her.

I turned and walked away. Steve tried to talk to me all afternoon, to swoon me, to convince me that he wanted me. That he couldn't turn her away in front of all of those people. It was important to save face. Perception was everything to his kind, he said. If we weren't in public, I would have punched him. No, more like I would have kneed him in the nuts. Actually, I would have done both.

Two days later I met up with his soon-to-be-ex-fiancé to tell her all about the man she was intending to marry. She fell to pieces right in front of me. Then she took my hand and thanked me for saving her.

From that day on I declared it would just be me the whole way. I would be the one to make my dreams happen. And I would happily live those dreams on my own.

CHAPTER NINE

Sebastian

It was a good day. We'd won all our games and there were no injuries. The younger horses had a good run and had followed our instructions without fail. I walked beside Frankie down to the truck.

"Well, that will make our boss happy," Amanda said from behind us.

"Yes, we have good scores to take into tomorrow," Juan said. "We should get into the finals."

Frankie was quiet. I glanced over at her but she gazed straight ahead. She didn't even look at me when she spoke. "You know, you guys can go. We can hose these last horses down and do the feeds."

It had been like this all week. Whenever I offered to help, she insisted she could do it herself.

"No," Juan said from behind us. "My dad taught us that we should serve the horses as well. Polo is a team sport."

She sighed.

We untacked the horses and walked to the wash bays, each entering our own bay to hose the horses.

Frankie was laughing beside me. Her laugh was hearty and sincere as if it were made just for her. It was real: no pretence, no fakeness. "Ruby, get off the hose."

Frankie was pushing Ruby back. The hose was lax in her hand. When Ruby stepped off, the hose went taut. It was pointing straight at me. Water squirted me in the face. I yelled and jumped back. Frankie's eyes widened as she stared at me, then her mouth quirked at the sides.

"Sorry."

I doubted that. "Are you really?"

"No."

"Well, then, neither am I." I pointed my hose at her and sprayed her with water. Her mouth dropped open and I aimed for that. She spluttered and laughed. Without hesitation she climbed through the bars, dragging her hose with her, and drowned me in water. I squinted through the unrelenting spray and plotted my revenge. She was close. Grabbing her by the waist, I pulled her against me. Then I shoved the hose down her top. She squealed as she tried to break my grip. I let her go and pointed the hose in her face for good measure.

I couldn't stop laughing. My sides ached. I also couldn't stop staring at her. Her wet t-shirt clung to her body, not leaving much to the imagination.

"Children, you're working with horses," Amanda growled. "You're lucky they didn't spook."

Frankie and I tried to contain our laughter but every time we eyed each other we started again. I tried to sober up when Amanda's stern face came into focus. Her normally round cheerful face was anything but.

"Sorry."

"Take our two horses. We'll finish yours."

· "Sorry," Frankie said taking a lead rope. "This is your fault," she said to Ruby who turned her head away.

We walked to the yards together still laughing. The way her entire face lit up lightened my heart.

"Excuse me, Prince Sebastian."

We turned to see a lady approach us and a man with a camera. She wore tailored slacks and a fitted shirt that high-lighted all of her assets.

"Do you mind if we do an interview with you? We've heard that you've travelled the world playing polo and would like to get your thoughts on the sport in Australia."

I would rather have stabbed myself in the eye, but refusing wouldn't be good etiquette. I turned to Frankie; her face had hardened. There was no sign of her laughter or glorious smile.

I nodded to the reporter.

Frankie came closer and yanked the lead rope from my hand.

"Oh, could you ask your helper to stay? It would be good to have some photos with the horses."

I turned to Frankie imploring her to stay. I hated inter-views. How had they figured out who I was? The media from Oleander barely showed any interest in me anymore. Being away from my sovereign land for over fifteen years had a posi-tive effect on my newsworthiness. My bodyguards appeared out of nowhere and stood to the side. Frankie joined them. The scowl on her face evident to the world.

That scowl was directed straight at me. Again.

CHAPTER TEN

Frankie

"You should have seen it, Mum. It was Prince Sebastian this and Prince Sebastian that. Her eyes couldn't have said 'take me' any more clearly," I said into my phone.

Amanda was making our dinner in the kitchen. Walking past I swiped some carrot she had just chopped. I moved into the lounge, chomping away. I put the phone down on the table so I could comb my hair while speaking.

I needed someone to listen to me. Someone who would understand how I felt. Amanda was not that person. When I told her about Sebastian and the reporter, she ignored my protests and dismissed me with a shake of her head. Mum wouldn't do that.

"I guess that's what happens when you're a handsome prince," Mum said.

"What? He's not handsome."

"Don't lie," Amanda said from the kitchen. "He's hot. The

way his wet shirt clung to his chest and shoulders could make any woman weak at the knees."

I fought my brain as it tried to wander there. And not just there. His breeches were wet too. I could feel my mouth starting to water. I let out a frustrated sigh.

"Do you mind? I'm not talking to you." I turned away from her and sat on the couch. "How would you even know he's good looking, Mum?"

"Well, since you've spoken about him for the last few weeks, telling me how infuriating he is, I decided to look him up."

I nearly spat out the carrot. "You googled him?"

"Yes. And I agree with Amanda, he's hot."

"Ha," Amanda said.

I ignored her and changed the subject. "He didn't tell her what she could say and what she couldn't say. No non-disclosure agreement for the perky reporter, only for us lowly workers," I said, leaning back into the couch.

"Now you sound ridiculous. I can't believe you're still going on about that," Amanda said from the kitchen.

"Will you stop listening?"

"I can't help it if I've got good hearing."

"Not good enough to hear how arrogant he is sometimes."

"You're carrying on like a pork chop." Amanda made eye contact and rolled her eyes. They must be the fittest eyes on Earth with the amount she rolled them. "Keep going, tell her the rest of your story."

I huffed. "And then she looked at me with pity and said, 'please ask your helper to bring the horses over here for a photo' and as I'm walking over, she says to the camera man 'make sure she's not in the shot'."

"That's rude," Mum said.

"Don't just end the story there. Tell her what Sebastian did."

"Will you shut up?" I turned to Amanda and saw her big smile.

"Tell her."

"What did Sebastian do, Frankie?"

"He said 'please don't be rude to my...Frankie. This interview is over'."

"Oh, that's class," Mum said.

"Class? He was going to call me his helper but caught himself at the last moment."

"And he called you his Frankie instead," Amanda said with glee.

I gave her the bird.

"Frankie, you need to give the man credit. He could have just continued with the interview."

I stood up and paced across the lounge room. The thick carpet drowned out the sound of my angry steps. I couldn't believe what Mum was saying. "You sound just like Amanda."

"Well, Amanda's right."

"I usually am," Amanda said.

"It's his fault I resembled a drowned rat and wasn't even presentable."

"So now you're saying you wanted to be in the interview?" Mum asked.

"No."

Amanda opened her mouth.

"Shut up."

She smirked instead.

"How about you tell me how the tournament went?" Mum said.

"Good."

"We won," Amanda called out. "Prince Sebastian scored most of our goals."

I sneered at her.

"So, he's a good player then?"

"I suppose."

"He and Juan are the highest ranked players we've ever had playing for us. They'll be a six by the end of the season," Amanda said.

I shook my head. "Do you want to have this call with Mum?"

"I already am."

"With such high calibre players, you should do well this season," Mum said.

"Yeah, I suppose."

"I think I'd like to meet Prince Sebastian."

"So you can fangirl over him? No way." That's all I needed. I imagine having a worker's mother fixated on him would go against his precious NDA.

"I want to see what's so bad about him. Why you need to spend a whole phone call speaking about him."

I could hear the smile in her voice.

"I'm going now. Thanks for your sympathy."

What the hell, I can't believe my mother sided with Amanda. Why couldn't everyone else see Sebastian the way I did?

CHAPTER ELEVEN

Sebastian

Juan and I were in the living room of our apartment. We sat side by side on the couch, our bowls from dinner on the table in front of us. The TV was on but I wasn't watching. I was having trouble staying focused.

"You should have seen her face when the reporter called her my helper."

"I didn't need to. You've told me a million times."

"You're right. Sorry."

"You like Frankie." It was a statement, not a question, but I felt compelled to answer it, anyway.

"What's not to like? She's an amazing horse person. She's always full of energy. Her smile lights up the day."

"Si, and her stare could turn water to ice."

"True."

"Have you noticed how it's mostly directed at you?"

I had noticed and I didn't know how to change that. Some days we got along great. We worked well together. Then I would say something, or something would happen like that damn reporter turning up, and the switch would flick.

To add to that, I found it hard not to touch her. I remembered dancing with her, holding her close. She had felt perfect in my arms. And those lips had been so close to mine. I had wanted to claim them then and there. But I knew it would ruin any chance I had. She needed to make the first move.

"Sebastian?"

What was his question? Oh yeah, the stare. "Yeah, I've noticed."

"It's not a good idea." How did he always know what I was thinking?

"I know."

I did know. We'd be leaving at the end of the season. We might come back next year, but who knew. And there was always that need to return to Oleander and fulfil my duties hanging over my head.

Juan patted my leg. "I don't think you do know."

"I do." I sighed.

"I've never seen you like this before. In four years, you've never looked at a woman twice."

"None of them were Frankie."

WE PARKED in the carpark near the office. Frankie was on the field exercising some horses. I smiled when I realised she was talking to them. She glanced over at us, then turned the horses and went to the other end of the field.

"You go ahead," I said. "I'm going to speak to Frankie."

"Sebastian."

"I'll be fine. Go."

Frankie, stubborn as always, stayed up the other end of the field. I stood and watched. She never paid me any attention. Stuff it. That reporter incident wasn't my fault, so she couldn't hold it against me. She couldn't keep holding the fact that I was alive and breathing against me, either.

I would not let her treat me this way. I marched across the field. She would have seen me coming but still chose to ignore me. She was taking the horses through their paces. I knew she was close to being finished when she slowed to a walk.

"That news reporter being rude was not my fault," I called out to her.

"I noticed how you never corrected her when she called me your helper."

"I'm sorry, Frankie. I was just in shock. I didn't even want to do the interview."

"Really *Prince Sebastian*, you seemed quite obliging to me."

"What was I going to say? No?"

"Why not?"

"Because that's not the way it works. If I said no, they would just hound me or make things up or start investigating you and all the other people I spend time with. I don't want that."

Frankie stopped in front of me. "Would they really do that?"

"Yes. I try to stay out of the spotlight. I like it that way. I don't even know how they found me."

She nodded. Her face softened. "How often does this happen?"

"Not often. I'm good at staying hidden."

I was lucky my bodyguards had convinced the reporter not to publish until the end of the season. Money won out, again. At least it would mean I could continue my life of anonymity.

Frankie started walking back to the stables, keeping the horses in check so I could follow on foot without too much effort.

"Aren't you used to it, being a prince and all?" Her voice had lost its harshness.

"No. I've not lived in Oleander for over fifteen years. Most people don't even know who I am."

She didn't reply. I snuck a glance at her, her shoulders had softened and she was no longer clutching the reins. When we arrived back at the stables, Frankie dismounted and held the reins out to me. "Can you be a good helper and hold these horses while I untack?"

I took the reins and bowed. "At your service."

Her phone beeped and she took it out of her pocket to read. "Juan has decided he wants to come to the sales with us on Saturday. Amanda wants to know if you'd like to come too."

"The sales?"

"Horse sales. More like an auction. We like to go and buy one or two horses we think will be suited to polo."

I wasn't going to say no to spending more time with Frankie.

CHAPTER TWELVE

**Frankie**

"Gosh, there are so many horses," Sebastian said as we walked by the pens. I could tell some of the horses had been there for a couple of days from the smell of urine. It was probably not such a bad thing for some of them. It meant they would have received the most regular meals they'd had in a while.

I stopped at a pen with a mare and foal. I shouldn't have. I should have put my blinkers on and kept walking. The mare's hipbones were sticking out and patches of hair were missing. I swallowed the lump in my throat.

"What's wrong with her hair?" Sebastian asked.

"It's rain scald. A bacterial infection causes matted scabs."

"That's terrible." Sadness tinged Sebastian's voice.

"An infection this bad will be painful. It's likely contributed to her being under weight as well as malnutrition and feeding a foal."

"Is it treatable?"

"Yes. But it's hard work. She'd need washing with a special wash, the scabs would need to be removed and then she'd need ointment or spray."

I glanced at Sebastian. He rubbed the back of his neck, his eyebrows drawing together.

"Will someone buy her?"

"Not likely. Unless a rescue comes forward."

He nodded. He didn't budge from his spot. I wished he would. I closed my eyes and wrung my hands together.

"This is the reality of horse ownership," I said, opening my eyes. "People blame the racing industry, but she's not a race horse. There are breeders out there who breed indiscriminately." I hated it. I hated this part of the horse industry which treated them and their future with such disdain. But it wasn't all about greed. "Sometimes people buy horses with the best intentions but find they can't afford them or don't know how to look after them. So, they are sold again."

Sebastian nodded turning his attention from me to the horse standing before us. The muscles in his jaw clenched.

"Then adding to that, the drought has brought a lot of good horses to the sales as well. Farmers have no grass and can't afford to buy feed." I watched the mare as I spoke, eagerly eating her hay. She paid no attention to us. "They keep their livestock for as long as possible hoping the rain will come but it hasn't come for years. Some towns have to buy water in. Farmers then have to drive into town to get their 1000 litre allocation. They can barely survive themselves let alone water their animals. For some animals it's too late. They're too weak to make it to the sales." I took a breath in to steady my voice.

Sebastian's face was stricken as he turned towards me. I

understood that look. He was from another country; he had every reason not to know how bad it was for our farmers. But some people in the city, our cities, don't care. They turn their taps on and water comes out. They flush their toilets without thinking twice. Out west people showered or washed standing in plastic containers to catch the water. That water is then used in the washing machine or to flush toilets. The water from the washing machines is used to water gardens, just so Great-Grandma's rose bushes from 100 years ago didn't die.

"There are lots of reasons for horses to be here."

Sebastian stayed by the pen looking at the mother and foal. Then he turned full circle looking at all the horses surrounding us. Pen after pen of horses. I knew how he felt. It was overwhelming. I'd often leave in tears.

"Come on, we have more horses to look at," I said, tugging on his hand.

"What will happen to them?"

"Most likely a dogger will buy them."

"Dogger?"

"They'll be taken to an abattoir to be slaughtered, humanely, for dog meat."

Sebastian stopped in his tracks.

"I know it sounds terrible but what's the alternative? These horses have to go somewhere. They'll starve to death otherwise. All I hope is that it's done humanely."

"Can you give me a minute?"

"Sure." I continued walking, avoiding looking in the pens and reading the info cards outside of the pens instead, all the while keeping an eye on Sebastian. He was talking to his bodyguards. No one would have known that's what they were. They wore jeans and t-shirts like almost every other person there so they blended in. Yes, they were well built but not so much that it drew attention to them.

He brought them to the pen and showed them the mare and foal. They nodded and walked away.

"You OK?" I asked when he joined me again.

"Yes, no problem, shall we keep looking?"

"Why don't we catch up with Amanda and Juan? I'm sure she has some horses she'd like me to look at by now."

I didn't want him to dwell on all of the horses that were unlikely to find a home. Walking at a fast pace, I didn't look anywhere but ahead, until we found Amanda. Even though Sebastian studied the pens as we passed, I didn't allow him to stop. It wasn't that I was indifferent to their suffering, I just couldn't save them all.

When we reached Amanda, she showed me the horses she liked and we chose four to concentrate on in the ring. She always chose ridden horses. And that was her prerogative. She was managing a business and had a boss to answer to.

"The unridden horses will be auctioned in their pens," I explained to Juan and Sebastian. "We may as well go to the ring and wait for the ridden horses to be paraded."

Amanda tilted her head quizzically at me. I widened my eyes and gave her a quick nod in the ring's direction.

"Right. We can get good seats if we go now," she said and walked away.

Sebastian and Juan started talking and I caught up with Amanda.

"What was that about?" she asked.

"Sebastian was having a hard time learning some of the horses have no hope of being bought."

She glanced back at them. "So, the prince has a heart, does he?"

"We all have hearts."

"Uh-huh. Nice to know you care about his."

"Shut up. I didn't want him to be upset. So what? I'd do the same for anyone."

"Uh-huh."

I clenched my teeth, refusing to engage in the conversation.

CHAPTER THIRTEEN

Sebastian

WE FOUND a good spot in the stands and waited. Amanda and Frankie discussed the horses again. I checked the entrance, waiting for my bodyguards to arrive. When they did, they gave me a nod before finding seats a few rows away. Relief flooded through me.

"What was that all about?" Frankie asked.

She never missed a thing. Not with the horses. Not with what went on around her. I wasn't going to lie to her but I didn't want her to think I was showing off or something.

"I asked them to organise a rescue to save the mare and foal, with an understanding I would sponsor them."

"You saved the mare and foal?"

"Yes." I turned to her. "I couldn't bear to think there was no chance for them."

She held eye contact with me. The intensity made every-thing else disappear.

"The chance that they would have been bought by

someone was very slim." I watched her lips move as she talked hypnotised by them.

"I couldn't risk that. I just wanted them to be safe."

She reached over and gave me a heartfelt hug faster than I could react. When she drew away her eyes glistened.

"I wish I could save them all," I said.

She gave me a small smile and nodded.

We sat close on the bench, our arms and legs touching, and spoke about each of the horses as they came through. My horse experience was limited to polo. But I learnt Frankie's was immeasurable. She had joined pony club at a young age and had competed as well. Nothing high level but enough to get a grasp of different disciplines. And then came her knowledge about horses in general. It was phenomenal.

"What are you looking for in polo ponies?" I asked.

"We usually look at horses between two to four-years-old."

"That's logical. There is an investment in time with their training. And if they are too old, they may be past their prime."

"Exactly," she said, giving me a smile. "And we try to buy horses around the same height so it is easier for you riders to move from one horse to another. And if they're the same height you don't need to change mallets over each time."

"And we need not adjust our swing."

"Look at this one coming through." We watched as he was ridden around the ring. He held his head low as he cantered. "He is on our list. He holds himself well and moves with intention."

He was a stock horse who showed great agility in turning as the rider rode him around the ring. I had no doubt he had the endurance needed in the polo arena. He left the ring after Amanda had successfully bidded and won.

"And this one," Frankie said, grabbing my leg to make sure she had my attention.

The paint quarter horse was a little underweight but boy he could move. The stop on him was impressive and his roll backs were beautiful, so precise and effortless. He would be an asset to the polo team.

After the sales they went to the office to pay and then we loaded the horses onto the float.

"I only bring the two-horse float now. I learnt early on that if I brought Frankie and the truck, we'd go home with a full load," Amanda said, digging Frankie in the ribs.

"Yeah, well, they all deserve a second chance."

A girl after my own heart.

CHAPTER FOURTEEN

Frankie

"W‌ELL, at least we don't have to wear heels this time," I said to Amanda as I walked into the lounge room.

She scrutinised me and frowned.

"What?"

"Couldn't you have dressed up a little?"

I couldn't see what was wrong with my boots, jeans and band t-shirt. "We're going to a pub."

"Yeah, der, but a little effort wouldn't go astray."

"What do you suggest I wear then?"

She circled me as if I were a specimen. This was ridiculous. "The boots are OK. The skin-tight jeans are OK. But that t-shirt needs to go. You need to show some cleavage."

I sighed and examined her outfit. She wore boots, a skirt and a low cut, tight midriff top. There was no way I was wearing anything like that. "I want to enjoy myself, not worry about every guy there staring at my boobs."

"If you've got them, you may as well flaunt them." She grabbed my arm and led me towards my room.

"I can choose my own clothing."

"Obviously not. And that ponytail has to go."

I pursed my lips. When we got to my door, she shook her head and made a beeline for her room instead. I slowed down as she pulled me along.

"Don't panic. I've got just the thing."

I stood in her doorway, ready to make a quick escape. Metal sounded against metal as coat hangers slid across the rail. I rubbed my sweaty palms on my jeans.

"Here, this will be perfect for you." She handed me a black lace top. I examined the length. It was decent, no midriff would show. And it wasn't low cut. I could deal with that. I pulled my t-shirt over my head and slipped the top on. It fit me like a glove. It may not have been showing any cleavage but my boobs were certainly evident.

"OK?" I asked her.

"Yeah."

I pulled my hair out of my ponytail and combed my fingers through it. "Happy now?"

"Much better."

I checked myself out in the mirror. I guess she was right. My long brown hair did look better framing my face, instead of up in the ponytail. The top was dressy but not too dressy. The black lace design hid my bra well. I didn't feel exposed. And I liked the way it accentuated my waist so you could tell I actually had one, unlike my usual polo shirts that hid it.

A knock sounded on the front door. When I opened it, I sucked my breath in.

I took in Sebastian in jeans and a black shirt. The top two

buttons were undone. His light brown hair stood out against the black, and his brown eyes appeared soulful. I swore that man could look good in anything. I tried not to imagine how his jeans would be hugging his arse.

He gave me a broad smile. "You look beautiful."

He must have learnt from last time.

"Thank you."

Amanda pushed me out the door and closed it behind us. I walked beside him to the car. One of his body guards was behind the wheel and Juan was in the passenger seat beside him.

"Only one bodyguard tonight?"

"The other one is meeting us there. Since that reporter the other week they want to stay close."

I nodded. I'd never thought about how much his freedom was affected by such random events. His bodyguards always kept their distance but never stopped watching. He must have been so accustomed to it that it never bothered him.

Sebastian opened the back door for Amanda and I.

"I'll sit in the middle so you have more legroom," I said.

I slid in and Amanda followed. As Sebastian walked around to the other side Amanda said, her voice soft so only I could hear, "That was nice of you."

"I was being polite."

"I notice how you get to sit next to him."

My skin bristled. "Do you want to swap?"

"Oh no. I wouldn't hear of it."

I crossed my arms and tried to keep my legs as close to Amanda as possible. I needed to remind myself that rich and good looking were not my type.

CHAPTER FIFTEEN

Sebastian

THE PUB WAS FILLED with noise and energy when we entered. We trailed after Amanda as she looked for a table. The bar, made of dark wood, ran along one side. The rows and rows of liquor behind it were well lit. The coloured liquid looked like jewels in the backing mirrors. People were seated on bar stools at the bar and at tall wooden tables. It was a big place but still had an intimate feeling. Frankie held out her hand to me and pulled me along. I was relieved. Her mood had changed when we had got in the car and I had been worried we were going backwards. When we found a table to stand at, she let my hand go.

"What would you ladies like to drink?" I asked.

"A beer please," Amanda said.

"I'll have a Russian Mule please," Frankie said.

"A what?"

"I'll come with you."

"Whiskey for me," Juan said. "And bring back a round of shots."

Frankie led the way. I was happy with that. Her shapely butt looked good in skin-tight jeans. I would much rather me be looking at it than anyone else. We got to the bar and she managed to squeeze in between two guys. One of them started talking to her. Or should I say her chest. I was about to intervene when she held out her hand to me and pulled me closer.

"I'm with someone." Frankie pointed to me.

The guy glanced behind and I gave him a smile. He nodded and resumed checking out the barmaid instead. Did Frankie mean she was here with me or that I was her wingman?

When we got back to the table, the band was on stage doing their final sound checks. The energy in the crowd lifted as we waited in anticipation.

Frankie handed me her phone. "I found this earlier."

The mare and foal were right at the top of the horse rescue's Facebook page. They'd travelled well and were in a yard for themselves. The manager said they were both friendly and had been loved by someone before they'd found themselves at the sales. When they searched for a microchip, they found the mare's vaccinations were up to date. They contacted the vet for more information and they found the owner had passed away and his children didn't know how to care for the horses. I sighed. It was good to know they hadn't been mistreated.

Frankie smiled at my reaction.

"How did they get this information in so short a time?" I asked her.

"Rescues have lots of connections. Vets are usually happy to share information about the horses with them."

"Doesn't that go against privacy laws?"

Frankie shrugged. "It depends on what they tell them. They don't need to give names. In this case the vet was probably the family vet and would have called the owners for permission first."

The trips to the bar were frequent. Luckily the line was long and it took longer to get served as the night went on, because I swear the shots got stronger each time. Amanda brought up a list of shots on her phone and the names got more and more interesting. Frankie made sure that I ordered the ones with names like Leg Spreader, Wet Pussy, Sex on my Face and Panty Man. Watching her laugh when I ordered was worth it.

We finished a round of shots when a song came on that infected the whole pub. It must have been an Australian anthem because every time the chorus came on everyone shouted, "No way. Get fucked. Fuck off."

Frankie laughed at the stunned look on my face. Then her face became serious and she stood in front of me.

"I always thought you were an arrogant arse. Like when you handed us those non-disclosure agreements to sign. You practically flicked them towards us like we were plebs."

"I was nervous. I hate asking people to do things because I'm royalty. Usually my bodyguards handle that sort of thing."

"And then when we had finished filling them out, you scanned them with your nose turned up like they were something you'd found in a rubbish bin."

"The whole thing was distasteful. All I want to do is play polo, not pressure people to do unnecessary things." I hoped she could see how genuine my words were. Surely by now she knew I was not that person she thought I was.

She reached her hands up to my collar and they drifted down my chest. I was lost to her touch. Apart from the hug at the sales, she had never touched me so deliberately before. Her mouth was so close to mine I could feel her lips move as she spoke. "I forgot to tell you how good you look tonight."

Before I could kiss her, she spun around, grabbed my hand and dragged me to the dance floor to dance to an upbeat song. She said something about Aussie culture, before turning her attention to dancing. Amanda and Juan joined us. I was glad Juan was there, because at least there was someone else who had no idea what was going on. Everyone, young and old, knew the moves except for us.

There were many moves I'd like to make on Frankie. Starting with kissing those delectable lips and finishing with... anything that got us naked.

CHAPTER SIXTEEN

Frankie

MY HEAD ACHED as I stood outside the office and thought about the jobs I had to do. The sun licked at my skin, making me warm and relaxed. Lucky it was a Sunday and we had nothing major to do. Going slow suited me just fine. Drinking and lack of sleep didn't go well together.

Tyres crunching the gravel in the carpark brought my attention back to the world. Turning my head slowly, I saw it was Juan and Sebastian. They were talking and laughing. Ugh, how could they have the energy to be so happy? Sebastian got out of the car and walked toward me with a tray of coffees. He held it out to me and I grabbed the one with my name on it. How did he know how I liked my coffee? We were the ones who got the orders for the players.

"Thank you."

I closed my eyes and drew in the rich aroma. It was enough to awaken my senses. I took another breath in before raising the cup to my lips. I let the bitter taste rest in my mouth before the tepid liquid slid down my throat.

"Francesca, why you no look so good this morning?" Juan asked.

I opened my eyes and took in Juan's big smile. They were both dressed casually in jeans, t-shirts and sneakers. They obviously had no intention of riding today. Maybe they were suffering...a tiny bit. One could hope.

"Oh, I don't know Juan. It might have something to do with those shots you kept buying."

"*I* kept buying? It was you and Sebastian who went to the bar."

How could I forget? For some reason I had enjoyed the moments alone with him. I liked the way he had looked awkward when he had to order the shots. I remembered enjoying the feeling of holding onto his arm as I laughed. The way he only had eyes for me. The way I told him he looked good because for some random reason I thought compliments should be returned. I looked down at my hands. The hands that had touched him. What if they had slid from his shoulders, down his chest and lower?

I shook my head. That kind of thinking would lead to nothing but trouble. That's what drinking does to you.

Juan laughed, took the tray out of Sebastian's hands, let Sebastian get his coffee and then headed inside. Sebastian stood next to me, sipping his coffee, looking out over the fields. "It's so peaceful here."

"It reminds me of the farm. You can just stand still and let the silence infiltrate you."

"Like you are realigning yourself before you face the world again."

We stood together in silence, letting the sun warm us from the outside and the coffee from the inside. It was moments like this that you could feel that everything was right with the world. The scenery was constant, the sky an endless blue. There were no outside pressures, no demands.

"What was that crazy dance we did last night?" he asked.

"The Nutbush?"

"Yes, that one."

"It's something that's been ingrained in our culture for decades. Kids learn it at primary school."

"Right." He said it as if he thought we were odd.

"If we hear those words *church house, gin house* we are out on the dance floor in a flash—weddings, functions, wherever."

Sebastian shook his head.

I smiled right back and bumped him with my arm. "You'll learn it after a couple of goes."

He gave me a crooked smile like he doubted he'd ever get it.

"Do you have dances like that where you're from? Crazy things that just make you, more you?"

"No, nothing like that dance we experienced last night. We have a waltz we dance at important functions, even weddings."

It didn't sound half as much fun, but I wanted to learn more about his home country. I turned towards him.

Before I could ask another question, he said, "What's on the agenda today? We thought we could help."

"I need to scrub all the feeders and water troughs. And mow the field."

"Mow the field, I think I could manage that."

I tried to imagine him on the ride-on mower. I smiled while I thought of him in shorts and a singlet, beer in the drink holder like my Dad or brothers would have. Dad would have his Akubra pulled down low to block the sun's rays. He always said mowing the house yard was an immense waste of time but a necessity to keep snakes away. He used it as a type of meditation: emptying his mind and then building the list of jobs to do in a logical order.

After showing Sebastian what to do, I headed over to the yards and watched him while I worked. Sebastian was on his second lap when all of a sudden, he swerved off course. What was he doing? Dodging something? He got to the end and turned the mower around. The same thing happened again. This time he waved one of his arms in the air as the mower went off course. He was yelling at something but I couldn't make out the words. He turned again and made his way back, constantly looking at the sky in front and behind him. Ducking, he was almost lying flat against the steering wheel while raising his arm above his head.

Shit. The magpie. I hadn't warned him about the magpie. It was spring and nesting season had started. He didn't bother Amanda or myself because he knew we weren't a threat to him. But he wouldn't know that about Sebastian. He would have seen Sebastian on a horse but not the mower, and to a magpie he would represent two different people. That magpie wouldn't give up until Sebastian left his territory.

Sebastian tried to keep the mower on track while he protected his head and eyes from the ferocious bird. Sebastian's words became recognisable as he careened closer: "Piss off, you stupid bird...I didn't do anything to you...Leave me alone...You're crazy..."

His hand waved in the air adding emphasis to his tirade. When he neared the office, he hopped off the mower and ran, half bent over, still protecting his head.

His voice carried to me as he ranted to someone in the office asking if all animals in Australia were crazy. He came out with a mop that he swung over his head and a big straw hat. He went to the garden. I watched as Sebastian picked up small branches and twigs and stuck them in the hat. Armed with his mop and strange headgear he made his way back to the mower and resumed mowing. He held the mop in one hand and swung it when he approached the stand of trees the magpie was protecting.

CHAPTER SEVENTEEN

Sebastian

As I CONTINUED THE MOWING, defending myself against the black and white missile, I thought about how my mother could be compared to a magpie. She was relentless. I recalled the conversation with her the night before. It went the same way every other conversation with her did.

"Sebastian, the time for you to return to Oleander cannot be put off any longer. You have been away for too long."

She paused. I imagined her pursed lips as she waited for me to comment.

"Your duty is here, not amongst those polo players you associate with."

I tried to hold my tongue. But failed. "I'm fully aware of that. It is the only reason you call me."

She didn't deny it. She was not interested in me or the life I had created for myself. Because for her, that life did not exist. She said, "My country, our country, is always at the forefront of my thoughts."

I knew it should be at the forefront of mine. But it wasn't. I doubted it would ever be. More of my life had been spent away from Oleander than in it.

"No more avoiding your duty to the royal family and your country. This will be your last polo season."

My last polo season? I couldn't imagine it. I didn't want to imagine it.

"Your body guards have been issued instructions for your return from Australia when the season ends."

The phone disconnected.

The thought of what she proposed was beyond depressing. Less than two months of freedom was all I had been afforded. It surprised me I had been permitted to stay away for as long as I had. University finished five years ago. I'd started playing polo straight after, touring the world, doing what I loved. That life would soon be over.

I stowed the mower and made my way back into the office wielding my weapons. Taking the steps two at a time I practically flung myself through the door. I needed to sit. In safety.

"That bird is freaking crazy."

Amanda held up her phone and snapped a shot of me. "I got it all on video."

I didn't care. I had survived.

Juan burst out laughing as I rolled my eyes.

"Son, that is no way to treat one of our native animals."

I swung around. There was an older lady and gentleman standing off to the side. My tirade had consumed me so much I hadn't noticed anyone else was there. The lady stood with her hand over her mouth, trying to conceal her laughter but her eyes gave her away. I recognised those eyes. They were just older than the ones that could swallow me whole.

I grabbed at the ridiculous hat on my head and pulled it off.

Frankie came bursting through the door and made her way towards me. "That has got to be one of the most hilarious things I've seen. Please tell me you got it on video, Amanda."

She was tumbling over her words, not even holding back her laughter, as she grabbed my arm, drawing my attention to her. The older man cleared his throat and her laughter faltered.

"Mum. Dad. I forgot you were coming." She went to them and hugged them tightly. They had no reservations hugging her in return. In my family, embracing one another was non-existent.

"Obviously having too much fun," her dad said. A broad smile appeared as he held her close.

"Frankie dear, are you going to introduce us?"

Frankie stepped back towards me. "This is Sebastian. He's one of our international players this year."

She was looking up at me smiling when Juan spoke from the other side of the office. "What am I? This thing you call chopped liver?"

Frankie stared at him surprised and perplexed.

"Juan, darling, you know you pale in significance when Sebastian is in her presence," Amanda said.

Juan and Amanda giggled like school children. A blush rose on Frankie's face. I shoved the straw hat and mop behind my back and stepped forward. I held out my hand for them to shake.

"Nice to meet you Mr and Mrs–"

"Jim, you can call me Jim," Frankie's dad said as he took hold of my hand. He held it firm and covered it with his other one. I glanced down. His shirt sleeves were rolled up exposing arms that were well tanned and muscled. When he squeezed my hand, the tendons on his forearms flexed. I raised my eyes to his. His steady gaze held mine before he gave me the once over. I had the urge to stand up taller. His wife elbowed him and took my hand from his. Her hold was comforting compared to Jim's, soft and warm. If Frankie had told them who I was they showed no indication.

"It seems that my Jim has forgotten his manners. I'm Margaret." Her hair was short and wavy, the same shade of brown as Frankie's, and I wondered if Frankie's hair would be the same if it weren't long. She took the battered hat and mop out of my hand and handed them to Frankie. "Let's go and talk about magpies."

Margaret took me by the arm and led me out the door with Jim following. I snuck a look at Frankie. She didn't move to follow. We headed to the dreaded stand of trees and stopped twenty metres away.

"You know, magpies are completely misunderstood. They only attack because they're protecting their territory."

"And their young," Jim said, his voice low and gruff. His stern expression reminded me of Frankie's. Although they both had cheery round faces, when they set their jaw, they looked intimidating. "Of course, human fathers would aim for a different part of the body."

I shifted feet as if that would protect my manhood. Margaret gave him a sideways glance.

Margaret continued, ignoring her husband. "See, now, we are just standing here posing no threat to him. But if you were on that mower, he would be swooping, beating his wings, clacking his beak, while aiming straight for your head."

"Don't pose a threat and they won't scratch your...*eyes* out," Jim continued low and ominous. He stood still and rigid, looking from the trees and back to me. I didn't know what part of my body I wanted to protect more. I needed to stand my ground. I wouldn't call his bluff because I didn't think he was bluffing.

"You sound exactly like Frankie. She threatened to castrate someone, to his face."

Jim roared with laughter and slapped me on the shoulder. "That's our Frankie."

"Like father, like daughter," Margaret said, rolling her eyes. I smiled. I had no hesitation in believing either of their threats.

He looked around and headed to one of the paddocks. "It's a good set up here. I'm sure Frankie would like a similar set up when she comes home."

"Comes home?"

"Since Jim had his accident, he hasn't been able to do much around the farm," Margaret explained. "Billy has been helping with all the farm work. Frankie came down here to work and send money home to help us out."

"Things are better now," Jim said. "We're getting back on track. Frankie said she'll do another season and come home."

I couldn't imagine the stables without Frankie. She injected life into the place. The horses loved her, and she had such a good relationship with them. We walked along the track made by the horses and quad bikes toward the paddocks. Horses grazed peacefully, paying us no attention as we passed. Some stood in the shade of the trees sleeping. None used their shelters.

"Where's home for you?" Jim asked.

"A small country in Europe."

"And you're the crown prince?" Margaret asked. So, they did know.

"Yes."

"Why aren't you there now? Doing crown prince stuff?" Jim asked.

I walked over to Brutus who was hanging his head over the fence. I patted his cheek, just the way he liked it. He breathed deeply and moved his head closer.

"Being crown prince isn't something that interests me."

"Scared of commitment?"

By George, that man cut straight to the core. I looked him in the eye.

"No. I just don't want to commit to the wrong thing." I shook my head when I realised what I'd said out loud, to Frankie's family. It was not something I spoke about openly.

"What do you want to commit to then?"

"Horses. Making their life better. I'd like to set up a polo horse rescue where I'd retrain the horses so they can go to new homes. The ones that can't be rehomed because they're too old or injured can live a happy retirement with me."

Margaret smiled. I couldn't make out if she thought it was some crazy plan or the opposite.

"Can't you do that as a prince?" Jim probed. "You'd have the means."

"My family don't support it. The money I earn playing polo will go towards buying land and getting everything I need."

"Your family don't support you?" Margaret asked, shaking her head.

"No. They believe my sole responsibility is to my country and my people."

"That was the responsibility you were born into," Jim said.

"I know." How could I forget? It had been drummed into me from the moment I was born.

"Our children always knew that they didn't have to stay on the farm," Margaret said. "Brady didn't. He went to university to study law and has a practice in town."

"Aren't they upset you're not at home fulfilling your responsibilities?" Jim said.

"My mother thinks it's a phase and I'll get over it."

"What do you think?"

"It's a lot to go against your parents' expectations but it's even worse to go against the royal family and an entire country." My patting slowed and Brutus rested his head on my shoulder. I moved my hand to his nose, giving long strokes. "If I could do both, I would suffer through the reign knowing I could do something important to me. But at the moment that appears to be impossible."

I hated thinking about it. That title had a firm grip around my neck. I tugged at my shirt collar feeling like it was cutting off my air, just as that bowtie at the ball had. As the title squeezed, my lungs would scream from the lack of oxygen and my breaths would turn to empty gasps.

"I know it sounds selfish," I blurted out. "Running a country is important and the people are important. And in the realm of things my happiness isn't important. It's my responsibility and I shouldn't shirk it."

The words stabbed me in the heart. I couldn't keep denying my destiny. I closed my eyes, wishing the realisation away. When I opened my eyes, Jim nodded at me and gave me a small smile.

"If you had a property would you have it set up like this?" Jim asked, changing the subject. I took a deep breath and turned to him. As we walked back to the office, I told them what I would do differently.

CHAPTER EIGHTEEN

Frankie

"For goodness' sakes, will you stop watching them and help me finish the paperwork for next weekend's game?" Amanda said.

"I thought they were just talking about magpies."

"Obviously they found more to talk about."

"But what?"

"Does it matter?"

I sighed. Of course, it mattered. But why? It was not like I was interested in Sebastian. That would be the stupidest idea I've ever had, and I've had some pretty stupid ones. He'd be gone at the end of the season.

And this was no time to be distracted from my goal. The farm and horses were what was important here. I could still run cattle like Dad did. It was a good business and did not require a lot of hands on work all year around, which would allow me to concentrate on the horses while it brought in an income.

I turned away from Sebastian and my parents and went to the desk. "Who's playing this weekend? Please don't say Andrew."

"No, he has the week off."

We went through the players. As Amanda was completing the nomination online Mum, Dad and Sebastian walked in, laughing like they were the best of friends.

"She is stubborn alright. Have you noticed that scar on her arm?" Dad said.

I peeked down at my left arm. The scar was a red line stretching from my front to back.

"She did that while fencing when she was eight. We told her to wait for her brothers to come back from mustering, but she thought she could do it without them." Dad smiled at me and it was like a warm caress. "She was straining an old wire, bending over it to get enough leverage because she was so small, and it snapped. Lucky the damn thing didn't slit her throat."

Mum joined in, "Any sane person would have come back to the house to get treated. But not Frankie. She tore the sleeve off her shirt, tied it around her cut and restrained the whole length of fence. Just to prove she could do it herself."

"When her brothers found her, she was leaning against the quad with her eyes closed wearing a satisfied smile," Dad continued. No matter how many times he told the story he still shook his head in amazement tent. "Her makeshift bandage was soaked through. The cut was so deep we had to take her to hospital an hour away to get stitched up. The whole time she didn't stop smiling."

Dad came over and ruffled my hair. They better not have been telling stories about me the whole time. At least my brothers weren't there. They'd be sure to tell all the embarrassing ones.

"We learnt early on not to tell her she couldn't do something. It was worse if we told her to leave something to her brothers." Mum came over and smoothed my hair back down.

Dad gave a clap of his hands and rubbed them together. "Where are we all going for dinner tonight?"

My eyes widened. What did he mean by all of us? Juan had been quiet the whole time, peering over the top of a magazine he was reading on the lounge. All I could see was his shock of black hair, olive skin and deep brown eyes. But that's all I needed to see to know he was up to something. He closed the magazine. Smirking at my reaction he gave me a wink. "There's this great steakhouse down the road. They have square dancing as well."

"That's a great idea," Amanda chirped in. "Frankie, you can show Sebastian your country dancing skills."

I rounded on her, my jaw set and eyes narrowed. Her smirk matched Juan's. Tilting her head to the side she dared me to say something.

THE RESTAURANT WAS busy for a Tuesday night. The smell of steak cooking made my mouth water. It was beginner's night and by the looks of it square dancing was popular. There were kids, parents and older people as well. The atmosphere was alive. People were talking and laughing. Music played in the background. As we ate our entrée, they had a dancing demo. The dizzying moves were impressive. I had no idea how they could remember them all. One dance was so fast I got lightheaded just watching it.

Sebastian leant towards me and asked, "Would you like to dance?"

"OK." My heart rate quickened.

We got up and he took hold of my hand, leading me to the dance floor. I glanced down at our hands thinking about the warmth his gave off. When he turned me to face him, his smile gave me a jolt. I was lost in it and those brown eyes and him. Thank goodness you didn't stay with your partner too long while square dancing.

Mum and Dad got up to join us, as did Amanda and Juan. We laughed freely when we lost our steps. We had a caller but that didn't help all that much. My mouth and cheeks hurt from laughing and smiling.

After Sebastian and I had done three dances we left the dance floor and returned to the table. Mum and Dad followed soon after. Their smiles lifted my heart. I wished they could be this carefree all the time. When I moved back to the farm, I hoped I could take some pressure off them.

"I hope you play better than you square dance," Mum said to Sebastian across the table.

"You should see him play. He rides like he and the horse are made for it."

"Sounds like you, Frankie. Sometimes you are more balanced on horseback than you are on your own two feet," Dad said.

"Frankie trains with me sometimes." Sebastian turned to me and gave me a smile. "She's good for someone with no formal training. Have you ever thought of playing?"

"I've got more important things to do in life than play polo."

Sebastian's face froze and he stared at the table. The silence stretched out until Mum got up and said, "Come on, Sebastian, let's have another dance before the mains come."

She gave Dad a pointed look when she got up. I watched her and Sebastian walk to the dance floor, both in jeans and button-down shirts. They looked the part. Before they joined the group, she gave his face a light tap, more like a caress, and said something to him. He responded with a smile and whisked her into a spin. Dad watched them for a moment before turning to me. His face was stern, like it had been the first and only time I'd ever lost my temper with a horse.

"Frankie, sometimes your pig-headedness lets you down."

"What?"

"That man out there is more than a polo player or a prince."

I stared at my father. I turned and eyed Sebastian's body-guards across the room. "Is he though?"

I sat back and crossed my arms. Dad's face darkened.

"Get off your high horse, Frankie. That man has nothing but nice things to say about you. And all you can do is be condescending towards him."

"Calling me stubborn is nice, is it?" My voice shook.

"Well, he's not bloody wrong." Dad's voice was hard. He shoved his chair back and walked away. I stared at my glass of water. The liquid was rippling, even seconds after Dad had left. It wasn't his pushing away from the table that caused it. My hands were shaking. I removed them from the table and stuck them between my legs. Tears stung my eyes.

What I had said to Sebastian was wrong. Why should it

matter if he chose polo as a career? It shouldn't. He worked hard at it. He was good at it. His position hadn't just been handed to him because it was the Sport of Kings and he was a future one. He cared about the horses, loved them even. He never treated them with malice and was always kind in his training. If that didn't make him a good person, what did?

He never big noted himself or droned about appearances. When he donated at the fundraising ball, he didn't tell us how much he'd donated. He didn't strut his stuff when he saved the mare and foal. He was nothing like Andrew or Steve or some of the other well-to-do players. He didn't scream for attention or throw his money around.

And yeah, he called me stubborn. But wasn't I? Even when he showed me how to hold the mallet, I didn't tell him I'd tried it and it was so much better. Like saying that was letting him win somehow. But it wasn't a game and showing appreciation wasn't losing.

The chair moved beside me and Sebastian sat down. I willed the tears not to fall but they came anyway. Sebastian reached under the table and squeezed my leg.

"Are you OK?"

I took a deep breath in and let it out shakily. "I'm sorry." Taking another breath, I peeked at him. His face was open and kind. He wasn't staring at me like he was expecting more. He gave my leg a squeeze which encouraged me to go on. "I'm sorry for always treating you like you are nothing more than a prince...or a polo player. I'm sorry for being rude to you." No point stopping there. "I'm sorry for not saying thank you when you showed me how to hold a mallet properly."

He smiled at me and my heart lifted. I took my hand from between my legs and rested it on his.

CHAPTER NINETEEN

Sebastian

Frankie's parents pulled into the carpark. I watched as Frankie met them on the porch. She listened intently and then gave her dad a big hug. He must have received good news from the doctor; they had probably cleared him to ride again. That was the news he'd been waiting for. They'd told us last night at dinner they were down here to see his specialist.

"Earth to Sebastian," Juan called out.

"Yeah?" I didn't turn to look at him.

"Have we finished practice?"

"Yeah."

I faced Juan. I couldn't ever remember hugging my parents like that. We hardly ever talked, let alone joked or had fun like we'd had with Frankie's parents the night before. I knew our family was an anomaly. When I'd met Juan's parents, they were all hugs and kisses. They had no problem embracing me as one of their own. Juan's father had taken me under his wing and shared his knowledge about training polo horses. He had worked with me side by side every day, imparting that knowledge. He had made me promise that when I trained my own, he would get first pick. I had agreed without hesitation. Why wouldn't I? We were family.

The only knowledge my parents wanted to impart was how to be a good royal. *It is your duty to set an example to our people.* Telling me what to say and what not to say. *Sebastian, you must hold your tongue. It is not your place to speak.* How to act. *Sebastian, that behaviour is not befitting of a prince.* Who I could be friends with. *This is not a world where you can befriend whomever you like. You have a place. They have theirs, and it is not beside you.* How to make sure I used the media to my benefit. *Sebastian, turn and smile, make sure they see your interaction with the people.* Even from a young age I hadn't been interested. My younger brother was the opposite. He loved it all. When we made appearances, I followed his lead. He loved everything about royal life.

When I was shipped off to boarding school in England, in the hopes I would get some perspective on life and embrace my responsibilities, I found a freedom I never knew existed. My bodyguards had still been there but I had bribed them with my allowance. We had an understanding that they would still be present but they would let me do what I wanted, within reason of course. It had worked in my favour when I had discovered polo. They would drive me to practice and to matches. Then I had started working at the polo stables and they would get up early every morning to drive me there.

My bodyguards were loyal and had never betrayed my trust. My parents would have had a conniption if they knew a son of theirs was working. When my bodyguards wanted to do something, I would let them off work. At those times I would promise to stay at school where it was safe. Those two men stayed with me through school and my polo career. But the necessity for me to pay them extra had died a long time ago. But I was not foolish enough not to know that my mother still influenced them. Not in our day-to-day lives. But she ruled with an iron fist and would threaten their future employment. I knew they had no choice but to return me at the end of the season. And my loyalty to them would not prevent them from doing that. They did not need to endure suffering because of me.

I often wondered why my mother had not hauled me back to Oleander as soon as university finished. Whatever her reason, it would not have been for me. There was some calculated benefit for her and Oleander.

Juan and I rode to the stables in silence and untacked the horses. As we were hosing them down Frankie came over with her dad.

Jim watched. "Ah, yes, I see what you mean now, Sebastian. It would be much better with a rubber floor in here. And the overhead hose idea makes sense. No trip hazard then."

Frankie looked between us. "Were you talking upgrades?"

"No. Sebastian was telling Mum and I about his dream property."

Her eyes widened but she didn't comment.

Juan walked over and took Brutus from me. "I'll take them back to the paddock."

"Make sure–"

"Yes, yes, I know. Give them a pat before I let them go."

"Juan, before you go. Margaret and I would like to know if

you and Sebastian would like to come to the farm after the season finishes," Jim said.

Frankie's eyes narrowed and I swear if she moved her head any quicker, she would have given herself whiplash. I could almost see her brain working overtime. Yet, she stayed quiet.

"Frankie usually has two weeks off and we thought it would be nice to have you all up there."

Juan nodded eagerly.

"We'd love to," I said.

"Excellent," Jim said, clapping me on the back. "We'll see you in a few weeks."

I would garner an extra two weeks' grace from my bodyguards.

CHAPTER TWENTY

Frankie

"THIS IS THE FARM," I said to Sebastian as we drove over the familiar thump, thump, thump of the cattle grid.

Fenced paddocks bordered both sides of the driveway. The grass was browning; the August rains hadn't come this year. Each year they seemed to come later and sometimes not at all.

What was Sebastian thinking? The scene in front of him would have no resemblance to his home. There were no acres of manicured lawns and perfectly maintained gardens. The fences were plain post and wire, not the typical white post and rail fences most people imagine when they think about horses. The land here was mostly flat, no discerning features to be seen. But it was my home and I loved it.

"Lots of land for horses. How big are these paddocks?" he said.

"These front ones are twenty acres. Good for small herds of four to five horses."

"Is the grass adequate for sustenance?"

"Horses or cows that are in good condition can live on this grass alone. We rotate the paddocks to let them rest."

He nodded and continued examining the landscape. It had been weird when we had set out for the drive with just the two of us. Amanda and Juan would join us in a week after they had settled the new horses which were due to arrive the next day. Sebastian's bodyguards weren't with us either. He had told them to have a break. The trip wasn't as nerve wracking as I'd imagined. It was the same old Sebastian sitting next to me. The one I'd spent nearly every day with over the past few months. Sometimes he'd ask questions about the passing landscape like Mt Bauple, the only real landmark on the highway. Other times he'd ask about the farm. Or we sat in companionable silence listening to the radio.

The house came into view. It was two-storey, wooden, with wide verandas. It was big compared to other farm houses. Big because when your heritage was part Italian, big families were a thing. Dad had stopped that tradition by only having three children.

"Wow," Sebastian said.

I peeked at him to see if it was a good wow. The smile on his face said it was. I stopped the car near the house and rubbed my sweaty hands on my jeans as I took a deep breath. What the hell was wrong with me? I didn't even want Sebastian here. What did it matter if he liked what he saw? Sebastian reached over, took my hand and raised it to his lips. The warmth of his lips on my skin was as shocking as the action itself.

"Right. OK. Here we are." I fumbled for the door handle and scrambled out of the car as soon as the door opened, disentangling the hand he was still holding. The gravel crunched under my feet as I made my way to the boot to grab our bags.

"Aunty Frankie! Aunty Frankie!" The voices of my two nieces squealed in delight as their small feet thundered down the stairs. As soon as their feet hit the ground, they made a beeline for me. Their small blonde heads bobbing as they ran. I lifted them each in one arm and spun them around. Giggling erupted.

"Aunty Frankie, do you know we have a foal? It was born this morning. We got to see it."

"Pop said it was a present for your homecoming. Oh." Tilly stopped talking and looked at her six-year-old twin wide eyed. "Oh no, we forgot. It's meant to be a secret."

"I'm sure I can pretend you didn't tell me."

"Can you? Can you really?"

I glanced at Sebastian who was watching the exchange totally bemused. Livvy and Tilly stared at him.

"Who are you?"

"Shoosh, Tilly. He's the prince. Remember Mummy said Aunty Frankie was bringing a prince to stay."

"He doesn't look like a prince." Tilly scrutinised him and then walked around him, nodding to herself. "Aunty Frankie, are you going to be a princess?"

Holy shit. Out of the mouth of babes.

Movement sounded behind me and I turned to see my older brother approach. I'd recognise that mop of wavy brown hair anywhere. He grabbed me tight and lifted me off the ground. He wouldn't let go no matter how much I pushed against his shoulders.

"Don't be ridiculous. Aunty Frankie could never be a princess," he said, his brown eyes twinkling.

"Why not?" Tilly asked.

"Princesses don't wear jeans and polos." He put me down and flicked my collar.

"He's a prince and he's wearing jeans," Tilly said.

"And a polo," Livvy said.

Billy turned to Sebastian and gave him a once over. "My sister seems to have lost her tongue. Same thing happened to her when you met Mum and Dad I hear."

Heat rose in my cheeks. "Sebastian, this is my brother Billy. We ignore most of what he says."

"You only ignore me when you don't want to admit I'm right."

Tilly was yanking on my shirt. I peered down at her. She raised her eyebrows and indicated to Sebastian. Six-year-old sarcasm. Great.

"Sebastian, this is Mathilda and Olivia."

Sebastian knelt on one knee and stuck out his hand. They shoved it aside and went in for a hug. As soon as they had finished, they took a hand each and led him away.

"It's alright," I called after them. "I'll carry the bags."

They ignored me completely. I shoved Sebastian's duffle bag at Billy and followed them up the stairs. Mum was waiting at the top. She hugged Sebastian.

Billy gave a lopsided smile. "We shall call this the Sebastian Fan Club Headquarters."

I rolled my eyes at him.

"I don't know why you're rolling your eyes. You're his biggest fan."

I grunted.

"Don't deny it. You've never invited a male here before."

"Ha. I didn't invite Sebastian here. Dad did."

"Deflection is the best form of denial."

"Whatever." I climbed the remaining stairs. Mum was leading Sebastian to his room. My nieces were still gripping both his hands.

"Look, Mum even gave him a connecting room. You can have secret rendezvous."

He turned his face back to the group ahead of us. I took it as my moment. I hip and shouldered him. It came as such a surprise he had no time to brace himself against the impact. He crashed into the wall. I rushed to catch up to the others before he had a chance to retaliate.

"You'll keep," he called after me.

CHAPTER TWENTY-ONE

Sebastian

MARGARET LED me to my room. It was painted a fresh, light grey. The window was huge, as tall as a person, and was open, letting a breeze in that fluttered the curtains. A wooden queen bed was set against one wall. Beside it was a door that Margaret opened to the adjoining room. "This is Frankie's room. I thought it would be nice for you to be close."

"I bet you did," Billy called from my doorway.

Margaret gave her son a withering look. "If you had a guest, we would put them close to you."

Frankie walked into her room and dumped her bag onto her bed. She gave her brother the finger. I had never witnessed such open hostility and love. Just like Frankie, her family was full of energy. My brother would never have openly joked in front of our parents. And the girls' unbridled enthusiasm would have been frowned upon. Sharing a doorway with a guest would have been unheard of.

Billy placed my bag on my bed and bowed. "Your bag has been delivered, Your Highness."

Margaret glared at her son. "Billy–"

"I'm sorry, we don't usually tip staff," I said, pretending to dismiss him.

He laughed. "This one's a keeper, Frankie. Come on girls, let's leave Sebastian and Aunty Frankie alone so they can get *settled.*"

Banging came from Frankie's room as she opened and closed drawers. The girls watched her from the open doorway. They didn't budge, even when Billy made his way out of the room with his mother following.

"Girls," Billy said.

"We want to stay with Aunty Frankie and Sebastian."

"Yeah, we can help them unpack."

"Let them have some alone time."

A slam came from Frankie's room.

"It's OK," I said to Billy. "Let them stay. We spent plenty of time together in the car."

Billy nodded and followed his mother out. I could hear Margaret scolding him down the corridor. The girls split up. I couldn't quite figure out which was which, even though they were dressed differently. Tilly, at least I think it was Tilly, walked to my wooden set of drawers that sat beside the wardrobe and pointed to the top one.

"Mummy puts our underwear and socks in the top drawer. It doesn't make sense to me. We use them the most. I think they would be easier to get from the next drawer down."

I opened my bag and grabbed my underwear and socks. "Can you open that drawer for me please?"

Tilly beamed. She opened the drawer and picked up the

socks I'd dropped. We continued like that, Tilly issuing instructions and me following them. Livvy and Frankie came and sat on my bed while we finished. Livvy spoke non-stop to Frankie who listened, enthralled by every word as if she were listening to a victory speech. She nodded and asked questions and used the most expressive facial expressions. Every now and then she would look over at me and smile.

As soon as I finished unpacking the girls dashed out of the room at top speed. They were like a whirlwind that took all the energy with them. I sank down next to Frankie.

"It's quiet without them," I remarked.

"I know. Let's enjoy it a moment longer."

I wanted to see her room, to see what it was like, to get a glimpse of her growing up. But it didn't feel right to go to the doorway and peek in.

"Are you ready to meet the rest of them?" she asked.

"How many more are there?"

"Louise, my sister-in-law; Noah, he's four; Sarah, who's three; and my other brother Brady, but I don't know if he's home yet."

"OK." How was I going to remember them all?

I followed her down the corridor. Light filled it from the skylight above. Everything about this house was bright and happy, just like Frankie. Well, just like Frankie after she decided I was no longer an arrogant jerk. Maybe it was that fact that had driven me to kiss her hand earlier. Maybe I thought that was a non-threatening way to show her I wanted to get closer. But her reaction left me in doubt.

Regardless of why I did it, that action, that opening I'd attempted to make, was wrong. I knew I'd be leaving soon. That I'd leave her and this life behind.

I turned my attention to the photos that lined the walls. Some appeared very old, black and white in worn wooden frames. I stopped to look at them one by one. Some people had the same features as Frankie and her dad: straight noses, full lips, rounded faces. An older photo caught my eye. A lady, older than Frankie, but with the same beautiful, unblemished skin and the same smile Frankie had when she was trying to hide something. She couldn't though, that smile gave her away every time.

"That's my great-grandmother, Francesca. She gave birth to eight children in this house."

"That's insane."

"I know. Dad says this house has always been full of life and love."

"Do you want a big family?" I peeked at her as I waited for her to respond.

She shrugged her shoulders and continued to look at the photos. "Mum jokes that the only grandchildren she will get from me are foals."

CHAPTER TWENTY-TWO

Frankie

I LED Sebastian into the kitchen. The open plan living area was the life of the house. It's where everyone gathered. The large kitchen window above the sink opened onto the balcony and acted as a servery when we ate outside. The view from it showed the stables and paddocks, all the way to the forestry beyond.

Mum beamed at us. She was in her element cooking for a big crowd. She loved having all of the family home. I turned to the dining table where the twins were arguing.

"I'm sitting next to Sebastian. I'm the one who helped him."

"That's not fair."

"If you two argue, neither of you will sit next to Sebastian," Louise said. "Now sit down."

They grumbled and each took a seat. Louise came over to us and embraced Sebastian. Poor Sebastian had probably never had so many people invading his personal space. In typical Sebastian style, he took it all in his stride. The only time I'd ever seen him lose that calm exterior was with Andrew or someone else who didn't treat the horses or the team with respect. Then, his distaste showed on his face.

"It's so nice to meet you, Sebastian," Louise said. "We've heard a lot about you. Mum and Dad told us all about their last visit. And Frankie always has a lot to say."

I stood frozen. What was she talking about? I didn't talk about Sebastian.

Sebastian smiled at me. "Does she now?"

"No, I don't." I made to move to my chair but Louise grabbed my arm. My death stare did not shut her up. She smiled at me innocently, her blonde pixie features showing nothing but sweetness.

"Sure, you do. It's Sebastian this and Sebastian that and Sebastian is so infuriating."

Billy walked in the room carrying a tray. "Why do you think Mum and Dad insisted on meeting him when they came down?"

I needed the floor to collapse beneath me.

Louise nodded. "Last week you were saying how well Sebastian rode and how he scored four goals in the final. Then you mentioned how he helped you with some fencing."

Billy piped up. "Frankie let someone help her? That'd be a first."

I glared at him.

"Actually, Frankie and I work together a lot. I'm happy to help."

Mum walked to the table with a tray of roast vegetables. Before Billy could say another word, she placed the tray in front of him and said, "Enough."

Billy smirked. I knew very well it wasn't enough. Not for him. He better get over it because I wasn't going to put up with his smart comments for the next two weeks. I didn't want Sebastian getting the wrong idea. I wasn't interested in him, and certainly not in the way they were implying. Dad came into the room. Sebastian stood up to shake his hand before Dad made his way to the head of the table, then we all sat. The smell of roast beef was mouth-watering.

I whispered to Sebastian, "We say grace at meal times. We need to hold hands."

Tilly offered hers and he took mine without question. A jolt shot up my arm at our connection. What was wrong with me? We were holding hands for grace, nothing more.

"Thank you, God, for bringing our family together. Thank you for providing us with this meal. But most of all, thank you for bringing Frankie and Sebastian home safely."

When Dad had finished, he stood up to carve the beef. Sebastian held my hand for a little longer. I let him. I liked the way his touch was firm, reassuring. What on earth? Reassuring? I shook my head and withdrew my hand.

"I like this big family thing," Sebastian said to me as the chatter started around the table.

"Don't you have big family dinners?"

"Not really. It's just my brother, Edward, and I, with our parents usually. We don't see our extended family often."

I was curious. He had never spoken about his family.

"Are you close with your brother?" I took the plate of roast potato from Louise. I loved Mum's potato, it was always crisp on the outside, fluffy on the inside.

"We talk and get along fine. But it's nothing like your family. We don't joke around or tease each other."

"Some people could tease a little less." I eyed my brother across the table. He was cutting the slices of roast into small pieces for Noah and Sarah.

"But you make it so easy for him. He knows he's got you as soon as your expression changes."

"I can't help it though."

"I know."

I was captivated by his genuine smile.

"Sebastian, tell us about some of the countries you've visited," Louise said.

"Louise worked her way around Europe for a year," Mum said, smiling proudly at her.

"I got to see some amazing places."

"But she missed me too much and came home," Billy said, giving her a kiss.

"And started my new adventure. The best one I could ever ask for." She leant down and kissed the top of Noah's head. It warmed my heart knowing she loved her family so much. I envied her sometimes. I would like to have a house full of love and laughter. But some dreams had to make way for others.

We talked through lunch.

"What's your home country like Sebastian?" Louise asked.

I savoured the beef, as I waited for his answer. It was rich and juicy and seasoned to perfection.

"Oleander is a fraction the size of Australia."

"Is it like other European countries? Does it have a high population?"

"Yes. Nearly as many people as in Australia." Sebastian shifted in his seat.

"That's insane," Billy said. "All those people in such a small place."

"Most people live in urban areas."

Knives and forks connected with plates.

"Do you live in a castle?" Tilly asked, she almost sat on the edge of her seat while she waited for the answer. I could feel the tenseness from Sebastian, like one of our horses preparing for a game.

"I did when I lived in Oleander."

"Is it a fancy castle?"

"Yes."

"Is the castle in the country? Is that where you started to play polo?" Louise asked. Perhaps she recognised that Sebastian was uncomfortable with the line of questioning. I silently thanked her.

"No. I discovered polo at boarding school. We had a polo team and there were polo fields close by. I loved watching the games."

"And then did you play polo?" Livvy asked.

Sebastian's smile stretched across his face. "No. At the time, I'd never ridden a horse in my life. I had to learn to ride first. Every day after school I'd go to the polo stables off campus and take lessons."

He only learnt to ride in his teenage years? He was such an excellent rider I thought he'd been riding for as long as I had. He would have worked hard to build the skill he had.

"And then did you play polo?"

"No. After learning to ride a horse I then had to learn the skills to play polo. It's one thing to sit in a saddle, hold on to your reins and go in a circle. Playing polo is a completely different thing."

"How?" Tilly said. She was hanging onto every word Sebastian said.

"Well, I needed to be able to hit the ball with the mallet. I practiced and practiced swinging the mallet and hitting the ball. Then came riding and using the mallet at the same time. I started on quiet ponies. Ponies that would listen to me and look after me while I continued to learn."

Sebastian's face glowed.

"How long did it take to learn all that?"

"From the time I started learning to ride until my first game was a year. The polo stables I rode for insisted that I be the best athlete that I could and would only let me play when they thought I was ready."

Billy nodded. I recognised the look on his face. He had determined that Sebastian deserved respect.

"Pop, are we going to show Aunty Frankie her surprise now?" Livvy said as I got up to help Mum clear the table.

"Why don't we all help Nan clear up and then we can go and show Aunty Frankie?" Dad said.

MY FAMILY TOOK the lead and Sebastian and I followed them out the back door. Sarah was in Louise's arms and she kept looking back at Sebastian. She gave him a big grin. Saliva ran down her chin and her cheeks were red. She must be teething again, even though she should have stopped by now. She erupted into giggles. Being behind Sebastian I couldn't see what he'd done to cause such a reaction. I studied Sarah's face; she was entranced.

My feet stilled when I walked into something and

rebounded. My eyes averted themselves from Sarah and I found myself staring at Sebastian's back. He took a step to the side with terror on his face.

"What's wrong?" I asked him.

He pointed. Our pet magpie. I bit my lip trying not to laugh. I failed. "That's our pet magpie, Nathan."

"You have a magpie as a pet?" He took another step away.

"Yes, Nathan has been with us for many years. His family live in that big gum tree over there."

Sebastian's stare stayed on Nathan, where he perched on the railing. Nathan peered back at him with his dull red eyes. Neither of them moved.

"Nathan won't hurt you. He trusts us. Mum will give you some mince to feed him later. Once you feed him, you'll be friends for life."

"Feed him?" Sebastian's wide eyes turned on me.

Poor Sebastian. I held his arm. "Yes, not by hand. You can put a couple of balls of mince on his plate. He will watch you do it. Then he will remember your face. He'll never attack you."

"OK." Sebastian sounded unsure. I smiled thinking about how much trust he had in me. We walked down the stairs together. Realising I still had hold of his arm, I let go. My hand felt awkward just hanging there at my side. I stuck it in my back pocket so it didn't stray to Sebastian.

Dad led us out the back to the horse paddocks. There were four horses I'd never seen before in the half-acre paddock and in a yard were a mare and foal. They were all underweight and their coats in poor condition. I looked down at their hooves, which were usually another clear sign of neglect. They were overgrown.

"Whose horses?" I asked.

"Yours."

I glanced between Dad and the horses.

"Someone asked if I could take them to the doggers. I couldn't do it. Not the mother and her unborn foal. Not the others, they were all so close. I couldn't split them up. So, I brought them home for you."

"Pop said you would know what to do," Tilly said.

"He said you could make them better," Livvy said.

"And could find them new homes."

Dad's smile was like a child who had bought his mum a box of chocolates from his pocket money. Sebastian was at the fence watching the mare and foal. They were both dark bay with four white socks. The mare had a white strip down her nose. Sebastian crouched and examined the foal suckling before turning to me. His smile was as big as my dad's.

"It's a colt. Smart one, can suckle both teats from one side already. It's got good legs, not contracted or lax."

I had a look. He was right. The foal was not on his toes or bumpers, meaning its tendons were good. And he appeared healthy for a foal born to a malnourished mum.

Sebastian walked to the gate of the paddock and waited for me. He stood with his hands atop the gate. I copied his stance when I reached him. Our hands touched and I felt a tingle. I knew he wanted to go in, I could see it in his eyes, the way he watched the horses. But he seemed to be waiting for me to decide. Like what I wanted mattered.

"Let's go in," I said.

As soon as the words had left my mouth, he opened the latch. We walked together, slowly, so we didn't startle the horses. They stopped grazing and watched our approach.

Sebastian put his hand on my arm to stop me. He was studying the horse at the back of the herd. Its eyes were wide and stance stiff, ready to take flight if we posed a threat.

I stood still beside Sebastian. As he slid his hand down my arm, his fingers grazed mine. I had a sudden urge to hold his hand, to steady myself with it. But that was ridiculous. Why would I need him to steady me, especially around horses?

One of the horses studied us. More curious than scared. She was chestnut with a white blaze and one brown eye and one blue eye.

"Hi, Beautiful. Do you want to come over?" I cooed.

The horse raised its head higher, took a breath in and blew the air out. She was taking in our scent particles.

"Good girl." I hoped she was a girl. It was hard to tell from this angle. She walked to us; her pace slow. The other horses paid close attention.

"You're so brave. We aren't going to hurt you."

She stopped. Not close enough for us to touch her, unless she stretched her neck out. I held out my hand. She brought her nose to it and sniffed. Deeming I was OK, she stood her ground. I opened my hand to pat her nose. My heart beat fast. She took a step closer and turned her head to Sebastian, allowing him to pat her.

"Such a pretty ranga," I said.

Sebastian side eyed me and laughed. "I'll never get over that term. How you get ranga from redhead is beyond me."

One by one the horses came over, even the skittish one. The flaxen chestnut was the only one who wouldn't accept a pat. His coat was a beautiful deep red and his mane and tail blonde.

"They're not wild," Sebastian said. "The boy, he's been gelded. And they all have brands."

I nodded. It wouldn't take long for them to get accustomed to us. They let Sebastian pat them one by one, except the gelding. Sebastian's voice and hands hypnotised them. I smiled. Him, the way he treated horses, his soothing attitude, made me feel content.

"Aunty Frankie, will they be our friends now?" Tilly called from the gate.

"Soon," I replied.

Sebastian gave the brave mare another pat before returning to my side. He took my hand as we made our way back to the gate.

"So, you're just like Frankie then? A crazy horse person," Billy said. He couldn't suppress his smile.

We followed Dad so he could give Sebastian a tour. Tilly, tired of walking, asked Sebastian if he could give her a piggy back ride. He carried her as if it were no effort. My chest expanded and felt light. Weird.

CHAPTER TWENTY-THREE

Sebastian

THE FARM WAS NOT pristine like the polo stables. It wasn't run down, but you could tell it was a working farm that had passed through generations. The buildings were older and weathered. Some of the machinery and implements inside the sheds were the same. Ploughs, or what I imagined were ploughs, were rusty. Some paddocks were fenced with old posts, and the wood had cracked and discoloured over the years. Other paddocks had new posts that had not deteriorated. The land stretched far into the distance, conveying a feeling of seclusion.

We stood next to the stables with Frankie's family. The two younger children climbed the railing fence. Their cheeky grins were just like their father's, as was their thick, brown wavy hair. My eyes constantly darted to them. I was worried about them falling. My attention was drawn away when Billy said, "Frankie, come over here. I want to show you what we did with the stable roof."

She stood next to him and examined the roof. Her face scrunched up as if she was confused. "What? I can't see anything."

Before he could respond she danced from foot to foot.

"Shit. Shit. Shit."

I followed her desperate gaze down to her feet. She was standing on an ant nest. These ants were bigger than normal ones; just like everything else in Australia seemed bigger. She danced away slapping at her legs before tearing her boots off. Then she ripped her jeans off. Standing there she slapped the ants away. Too stunned to move, all I could do was watch. Billy roared with laughter.

Louise made her way to Frankie. "Geez you're a shit-head," she said to her husband.

"She asked for it."

"Really? I doubt she asked to be attacked by ants."

"For goodness sake, Billy. You couldn't even last half a day," Margaret scolded.

Frankie picked up her boots and hurled them at her brother, each one connecting with enough force that he winced.

"I told you you'd pay." He was still laughing. Turning to me, he said, "Stop staring at my half naked sister."

It had all happened so fast it didn't register that Frankie was standing in front of me in her underwear and t-shirt. But now I was admiring the shape of her toned legs and butt. Her legs were well tanned from where her work boots would have ended up to what would be her shorts line. I dragged my eyes away.

"I couldn't help but notice her tan line."

"Yeah, as if that's all you noticed." He clapped me on the

back. He walked away with his wife following, telling him off for starting an all-out war. As he smiled and I had the feeling that's exactly what he wanted.

Everyone followed until it was just Frankie and I left standing beside the stable. She had her jeans inside out and was shaking them. I retrieved her boots and handed them to her.

"Thanks."

She put her jeans and boots on.

"Is it always like this? People and chaos and crazy antics."

"Not always. Sometimes we can be civilised."

"I prefer the madness."

Her head snapped up.

"Can you imagine a home with no fun or laughter? Where all rules had to be followed?" I asked.

She shook her head.

"My home is twice as big as yours, but filled with not even half the love."

"Only twice as big?" she asked as she walked towards me.

"Well, OK, it's a castle. This is no time for semantics."

"Didn't you do things with your brother? Play games? Ride bikes?"

"No."

"What about cops and robbers? Or hide and seek?"

"No."

"That sounds awful."

She took hold of my arm and led me away from the others. "I want you to meet someone."

We walked through a gate near the stable. A brown horse was there waiting for us and as soon as she saw Frankie she nickered. The horse trotted over to Frankie who scratched her ears. She turned to me, smiling. "This is Jane. I've had her since I was eight. She's my best friend."

Frankie walked around the mare, examining every inch of her. She lifted the mare's feet to check them and inspected her mouth. Then Frankie lifted her finger and Jane lifted her lip giving us a smile.

"Come closer," Frankie said.

I did as she asked and patted Jane. Her nose was soft and warm and she liked resting it in my palm. Her breath made her whiskers move, tickling my hand.

"Jane, give Sebastian a kiss."

She lifted her nose out of my palm towards my head. When her lips reached my cheek, she twitched them, brushing my skin. I wished they were Frankie's lips but I had to take what I could get, and if Frankie liked me enough to let her horse kiss me that was a step in the right direction.

"Good girl, Jane." I patted the length of her nose and gave her a kiss on her cheek.

"She likes you," Frankie said. "We'll go for a ride soon, I promise," she said to Jane before giving her a final pat and walking out the gate.

"At home, what did you do for fun?" Frankie said, resuming our previous conversation.

"We didn't really have fun."

She was quiet. I looked down at her and she gave me a sad smile.

"I read a lot. Those books took me to amazing places and on terrific adventures. Harry Potter was a favourite."

We stopped walking and she turned to me. Reaching up she pushed the hair out of my eyes. Her touch left heat behind.

I continued, "When I went to boarding school, I found a freedom I never knew existed. It was like everything pressing down on me disappeared. And then I found polo and horses. They showed me love and kindness."

It sounded terrible when I said it out loud. I gazed out towards the horses.

"I don't mean that my parents didn't love me. They do. But there were always expectations, and I did nothing but fail them."

Frankie drew me in close and hugged me. I tried to relax in her arms, but the past held on and the future pressed in on me. "I never want my children to feel like that. Like my love for them has to be earned."

I closed my eyes and rested my head on hers. I breathed in roses and vanilla. I imagined the scent travelling through my cells, reducing the tension in my muscles as it passed through. As I relaxed, other senses wakened. Frankie was soft in my arms, her breasts pressed against my chest. I pulled her in closer. Her steady breathing hitched.

I wanted her. All of her. I wanted those strong legs wrapped around me. Skin on skin. Lips against lips.

Frankie pulled away. "I'm happy to give you Billy. He'll make your life a lot of fun."

Her smile emboldened me. I bent my head and brushed my lips against hers. I held my breath expecting her to pull away.

CHAPTER TWENTY-FOUR

Frankie

Warmth spread through me as my lips returned his brief kiss. I wanted more…just a little more. Those brown eyes held me, trapped, and I didn't care. My heart rate picked up pace. I moved in closer.

Running footsteps approached us.

"Aunty Frankie, Aunty Frankie, Mum and Dad said we could stay tonight." Tilly launched herself at me and I stumbled from the force.

They chattered at us as we headed back to the house. I wasn't listening. I touched my fingers to my lips. Why had I returned the kiss? I must have been lost in the moment. Hours ago, I couldn't get away from him fast enough when he'd kissed my hand. I found myself watching his lips as he smiled, wanting more.

I shook my head. This wasn't right. I must have felt sad for him when he told me about his family. My emotions must have been confused.

Tilly's voice broke into my thoughts. "This is the dunny."

"It's an outside toilet," Livvy explained. "It doesn't even flush."

Sebastian's eyes narrowed as he considered it.

"We still use it," I said.

The girls turned to me wide eyed. I gave them a wink. "Well, the boys use it when we have a full house. Sometimes the inside toilet is being used by the girls."

Sebastian glanced between it and the house deep in thought.

"But, Aunty Frankie–"

"Not what you expected out here in the country? I guess it doesn't compare to your golden throne."

"Aunty Frankie–"

"Come on girls, let's go upstairs. It looks like Pop is waiting for Sebastian."

Sebastian glanced at the dunny one more time before making his way to Dad and Billy. The girls ran upstairs and joined Louise and Mum at the table on the wide veranda. I sat next to Mum and watched the three men talk.

"Sebastian's nice," Louise ventured.

"Yes."

"He's been in Australia all season?"

"He came before the season started, so about six months. Why?"

"Oh, just wondering."

"Don't bother getting any ideas. He'll be off again soon."

"Really?"

What was she suggesting?

"He has a home to go to, you know."

"Oh, that's right. The castle."

"Yes, the castle."

I gave her a look hoping she'd drop the subject.

"Frankie, he hasn't been there for a long time," Mum said.

"That's probably why he doesn't sound much like a prince. He's spent too long away from the royal family," Louise said.

The men were still deep in conversation. Dad was pointing toward the tree line in the north. That was the direction of the forestry where we had some of our cattle agisted during the year.

"I'm fully aware of that, Mum. The last time he visited was three years ago."

"I don't think he wants to go back."

"Do you really think he has a choice? He's the crown prince."

"Are you going to live in a castle, Aunty Frankie?" Tilly asked.

"Can we come and visit?" Livvy added.

"I'm not going anywhere."

"But–"

"This is my home."

The men turned and looked up at us. Then Sebastian walked towards the dunny. I couldn't wait for him to open the door, step in and realise he'd walked into a makeshift garden shed.

"Frankie, where's Sebastian going?" Mum asked.

"To use the toilet."

I watched as he got closer.

"That's not a toilet." Mum stood up.

"I told him it was."

Mum turned to me, her eyes wide, her mouth in the shape of an O. "Frankie, a huge snake lives in there."

I launched to my feet, my chair crashing to the ground. Running to the stairs, I called Sebastian's name. He was only metres away from the dunny. My feet moved as fast as they could down the stairs. My heart beat double time. I launched myself off the third step.

"Sebastian!"

He was at the door. His hand reached for the handle. I ran across the grass.

"Sebastian. Stop!"

He turned to me, surprise on his face. His hand was on the handle, turning it slowly.

I sprinted the last few metres. He was ready to pull the door open. Breathing hard, I reached him. I took hold of his hand and removed it from the door handle.

"Don't...go...in there," I said, panting hard.

"I need to go to the toilet."

"Not...there." I tried to breathe deeply but my lungs felt like they didn't have the capacity. I held onto his arm.

"What? You said to go here."

"Not...safe."

"What?"

"Snake."

Billy and Dad laughed. They were right behind us. I'd been so focused on saving Sebastian that I didn't hear them approach.

"I've never seen you run so fast," Dad said.

"I doubt she'd run that fast if it were one of us."

Sebastian gave me a crooked smile. "Sorry."

"For what?" I stood up straight.

"The joke's on you, sis. We heard you tell Sebastian to use the dunny."

I looked between them uncomprehending. I dropped hold of Sebastian's hand.

"Dad texted Mum to clue her in. She came up with the snake story."

I peered up at the balcony. Mum and the others stood at the railing, watching. Dad got a text. He smiled up at Mum and gave her a thumbs up.

Sebastian moved closer to me. My skin tingled in anticipation of his touch. I couldn't believe my own damn body betrayed me. He smiled. "Got you."

"Don't start a war you can't finish." I turned and walked back to the house. With my back to them I smiled to myself.

CHAPTER TWENTY-FIVE

Sebastian

"Sebastian."

I opened my eyes and stared up at the ceiling. I could faintly see the white wooden boards and the ornate ceiling rose. Muted moonlight filtered through the curtains. I was at Frankie's house.

Silence, except for, "Sebastian."

I turned to the whispered voices. The twins were standing beside the bed. What were they doing in here? I pushed myself up onto my elbow. That was an invitation to the two girls. They came closer and pressed themselves against the bed. I glanced at Frankie's door. It was still closed.

"It's too early to get up," I said

"We can't sleep."

"Why can't you sleep?"

"I don't know."

"We just can't."

Their voices were louder with each sentence. I heard

movement through the wall as if Frankie was tossing. If they kept going like this the whole house would be awake.

I lowered my voice to a whisper. "If you go back to bed and close your eyes, sleep will come."

"No, it won't."

"We don't want to go back."

Their voices were even louder. I sighed and patted the bed. "Hop in, let's go back to sleep."

Instead of walking to the other side of the bed they climbed over me. Elbows and knees dug in. Giggles erupted as they pulled the covers aside, got themselves comfortable and covered themselves.

"Sleep," I said, my voice firm.

The giggles subsided. I closed my eyes. They were tossing and turning. A dramatic sigh and then silence. Legs crossed over to my side of the bed. Cold feet pressed against my back. This was not going to work.

I slipped out of bed and approached Frankie's door. And paused. Looking back at the bed I saw that the twins had already taken over the entire space. I knocked softly and opened the door.

No going back now.

"Frankie?"

She stirred; her eyes opened slowly.

"My bed has been taken over."

"What?"

"The twins. They're in my bed."

Frankie's sleepy eyes regarded me.

"There's no room for me."

"Oh." She moved the covers aside and moved over. I hopped in beside her. "Thank you."

The only response I received was a grunt. I wished I could move closer to her so I could feel her against my skin. Instead, I covered myself in the covers she had been snuggling into only moments ago. I rolled over onto my stomach. Frankie's pillow smelled of roses. I closed my eyes encapsulated by her smell and warmth.

I AWOKE SLOWLY. Something pressed against me and when I opened my eyes and turned my head, I realised it was Frankie. She must have moved into me unconsciously. But I enjoyed her touch just the same. I wanted to turn on my side and wrap my arms around her. To hold her close with her willingly melting into my body. I rolled onto my back instead, making sure when I settled that she was still pressed against me. She stirred but didn't wake. I should have gotten out of bed. I shouldn't have taken advantage of the situation.

But I was a weak man. A man in love with someone who still wasn't sure about her feelings.

The longer I lay there next to her, feeling her body against mine, the more the realisation washed over me. I was in love with Frankie.

What was I doing? I wasn't even supposed to be here. By now I should have been back in Oleander. And instead I was opening my heart up to the biggest joy, and in turn, despair it would ever feel.

Small feet padded into the room. I turned my head towards the grinning twins. I raised a finger to my lips.

"Aunty Frankie is still asleep." I made a move to get out of bed. The girls launched themselves onto the bed, knocking the breath out of me, before rising to their knees and throwing themselves at Frankie. A gasp escaped her lips as they pushed the air out of her lungs. She was instantly awake. She grabbed Livvy and tickled her relentlessly. Squealing filled the room. When Livvy was rendered incapacitated, she turned to Tilly and gave her the same.

The door opened and Margaret walked in. Her pause when she spotted me was almost non-existent. All three females in the bed were in fits of giggles. I sat up.

"Dad and I want to go into town after breakfast. Can you watch the children please?"

"Sure," Frankie said, sitting up and making her way across the bed to sit beside me. She peered at me, pondering. Pondering what, I had no idea.

CHAPTER TWENTY-SIX

Frankie

I THOUGHT Sebastian joining me in bed had been a dream up until the moment I sat beside him. It felt natural, something two friends would do. But did I really think of him as just a friend? You don't move closer to friends when you think you're dreaming. You don't kiss them, even if you felt sorry for them. But it's not like it was a passionate kiss, it was just our lips joining for a brief moment in time.

What was the point anyway? He would be gone soon, back to his castle in a foreign land. And I would be here, at the farm I loved, living the dream I'd wanted my whole life. The dream I'd been working towards for the past five years. I had only one polo season left, and then I could be here full time.

"Are you alright?" Sebastian asked, his head cocked to the side.

"Never better." I forced a smile. I needed to cast these confusing thoughts away. I was happy with my life. I knew where I was heading. There was no need to complicate things.

Sebastian got up and headed to his room. "I'm going to shower."

I followed the girls to the kitchen. They sat on stools at the bench next to Noah and Sarah. I bent to kiss them each on the top of their heads. Sarah turned and planted a sloppy kiss on my lips, her eager hands squishing my face. She couldn't fool me. I knew she was trouble.

"The coffee machine is ready if you want to make Sebastian and yourself a coffee," Mum said.

"Good idea. He'll need it after his bed was stolen by two little munchkins before the sun rose." I hoped Mum would get the message that we hadn't gone to bed together.

The twins giggled. "We knew you would have told us to go back to bed."

"So, Sebastian was the soft target."

"Uh-huh."

I shook my head at their six-year-old cunningness and got the cups out for our coffee.

"Dad's already done the feed run. He's just been giving the new mob hay. He'd like to know what you need from the feed store."

"How much hay do we have?"

"We don't need any more yet. We can do a hay run in a few weeks."

I walked over to the coffee machine. Not one of those that created waste when you used pods. It was an Italian one like what you would find in coffee shops. After setting the machine to pour two coffees, I looked out the window at the horses. "Have they been eating well?"

"Yes, we've been giving them small amounts every few

hours and building up. And they have plenty of grass in the paddock."

I nodded. That was good. I'd noticed their poo was solid yesterday and there was no evidence of scouring.

"We probably don't need anything extra yet. I can go into town in the next couple of days with Sebastian to see what the feed shop has."

On cue Sebastian walked into the kitchen. His wet hair hung lower than usual. He gave me a broad smile as I put his coffee down on the counter. "Thanks."

He sat on the stool next to Noah who immediately climbed into his lap. Those kids had no boundaries. Sebastian shuffled backwards to make sure Noah was sitting properly.

"Toast or cereal?" I asked.

"Toast," Noah declared.

"You've already had breakfast," Mum said.

"More toast. I'm hungry."

"Noah–"

"More toast." His voice escalated.

There was no way we were going to have a good morning if he had a meltdown. I knew Sarah would react in response.

"How about you share my toast?" Sebastian said.

Noah nodded. "Baston and me have toast together." He slapped the counter top for added emphasis.

Crisis diverted. For someone who didn't have kids in his family he sure seemed to be in tune with them. Maybe it was something you learned as a prince, to have understanding for those around you.

He took a sip of his coffee. "Mmm, great coffee."

I smiled at him. A man who appreciated good coffee was a

man worth...Worth what? Keeping? Just because of coffee? That was ridiculous.

Mum wiped her hands on the dish towel. "Dad and I will be back by lunch time. Call if you need anything."

"I'm sure we can manage."

"Four kids, a few hours, what could go wrong?" Sebastian said.

Mum smiled that special mum smile and left the room.

I made toast for everyone and we sat down to eat together. Unsurprising, the twins chattered the whole way through.

"Can we go out and see the new horses after breakfast?"

"Can we play with the new foal?"

"Can we name it?"

"Can we name them all?"

"Whoa. Slow down," Sebastian said, laughing.

"Yes, we can go out after breakfast. How about I have a shower while you help Sebastian with the dishes?"

I stood up to put my dishes in the sink.

"Yay. I'll do the washing."

"You always do the washing."

"Do not."

"Do so."

"How about I wash and you dry and put away?" Sebastian said.

"Have fun with that. I'm going to shower." I patted his shoulder on the way past.

Before the arguments started again, I fled the kitchen. There was movement from behind me. I turned to see Noah hopping off Sebastian's lap.

"Aunny Frannie, I come with you."

I held out my hand and he ran towards me. His chubby

little hand met mine and we walked to the bathroom together. I sat Noah in the bath and got some toys out of the bag for him to play with while I showered in the adjacent shower.

As the hot water poured down on me, my shoulders relaxed. Noah played quietly in the bath, happy to race his cars around the rim. I thought of Sebastian with the three girls. I couldn't leave him alone for too long. They'd run rings around him. I sighed and turned the water off. Wrapping myself in a towel, I went over to the bath to lift Noah out. He clung onto the car in his hand.

An almighty crash came from the direction of my bedroom. I ran with Noah in my arms to my room. Sarah sat on the floor surrounded by drawers and clothes from my dresser. I put Noah down and ran to her. She looked up at me, her eyes as wide as saucers. I crouched and examined her. No bumps or bruises. My heart felt like it was beating so hard it would break through my ribcage.

Sebastian ran into the room. He examined the destruction, his head moving from side to side. As he bent down next to me and reached for Sarah, his hand was shaking.

"Aunny Frannie, drawers fell."

"Oh God, Frankie, I didn't even see her leave." He sat on the bed as white as a sheet. Glancing at the doorway, I saw the girls standing there with Noah.

"You've really done it this time," Tilly said to Sarah.

Sebastian swung his head around.

"She always does stuff like this," Tilly said.

I should have known better than to leave him alone with the three girls, especially Sarah.

Poor Sebastian, the look of horror on his face made me laugh. The shock of finding Sarah surrounded by a hundred things that could have hurt her, the relief of seeing she was OK, combined with the look on Sebastian's face made me laugh harder. I couldn't stop. Tears streamed down my face.

"I'm glad you think it's funny." Sebastian was smiling down at me. I wiped the tears from my face trying to sober myself. I stood up and made my way to the chest of drawers, pushing it back into place.

"How did this happen, Sarah?"

"Me wanted dancing box."

I knew what she meant immediately. My grandmother's old jewellery box with the musical ballerina. "Did you climb the drawers?"

She nodded, her bottom lip pouting. Oh no, I wasn't letting her start the waterworks with me.

"OK everyone, let's get this tidied up." I pushed the two bottom drawers back in and turned to pick up an upturned one.

"Maybe you should get dressed first," Sebastian said.

I looked down at my towel. It covered all my bits OK, but probably not when I'd bent down. Heat rushed to my face. So many lines were open to him but he chose not to say any. He let his sheepish smile say it all. I grabbed some clothes and went to his room.

"Aunty Frankie likes her bras and undies in the top drawer," Livvy said.

Could it get any worse?

CHAPTER TWENTY-SEVEN

Sebastian

"I LIKED that black lace bra of yours," I whispered to Frankie as we walked towards the horses.

I was repaid instantly. She grunted, gave me the finger and picked up speed so she was in front. That was perfectly fine with me. I liked the view.

"Do you think you could manage to look after the kids while I go in with the mare and foal?" Her attempt at sarcasm failed when she couldn't hold back her smile.

"I'll try."

"Aunty Frankie, can we come in too?"

"Not this time, sweetie. The mummy doesn't know us yet. We don't want her to get scared or angry."

Frankie shut the gate behind herself and stayed still.

"Then why are you going in?"

We stood at the fence and watched. I rested my hand on Tilly's shoulder. She looked up at me.

"Aunty Frankie knows what she's doing. See how she's standing as still as a fence post?"

Tilly nodded.

"She's showing the mum that she means no harm."

The foal was curious. As soon as he realised Frankie was there, he made his way over. I glanced down beside me to check on Noah. He was no longer standing there. Adrenaline shot through me as I turned around to find him. I let out a sigh when I found him playing with his cars a few feet away. I put Sarah down next to him and returned to the fence.

"Frankie is letting the foal come to her. Look at the mummy. She's keeping a close watch. But she is not moving to block the foal from Frankie and she's not calling it back either. And look at her ears. They're not pinned back which means she isn't angry."

"Can Aunty Frankie see all of this even though she's concentrating on the foal?"

"A good horseperson notices everything."

The foal nudged Frankie with his nose. Frankie laughed quietly and reached out her hand to stroke it. The mare showed no signs of concern. She just stood and watched. When the foal flitted away, she approached Frankie. I turned towards the younger children. They were still in the grass playing with the cars. When I looked back, Frankie was patting the mum and examining her from head to tail.

"Her teeth need doing."

"Yeah, I've doubt they've had their yearly dentals. What about worming?"

"Not yet. They should gain some condition first."

Both girls looked up at me for an explanation, I presumed. "If there are lots of worms, the horses could die from internal bleeding or colic if we try to worm them. We need the horses to be stronger first."

We turned back to Frankie, and she said, "The horses are just getting used to being fed again. We are increasing their feed very slowly so their stomachs learn to digest their food again. If we worm them on top of that it might cause too much stress."

That was a much better explanation.

She gave the mare a last pat and left the yard.

"Can we go with you to see the other horses?" Livvy asked.

"Yes, but you have to stay with me and do exactly as I say."

They both nodded. I watched as they walked hand in hand. Frankie was great with the kids. She didn't merely tell them what to do but explained everything so they could understand. And they paid attention to every word. Each time they looked at her there was complete adoration on their faces. I wondered if mine was as evident as theirs.

Sarah and Noah were no longer playing quietly. They were crashing their cars together with such force inevitably one of them would soon get hurt.

"Do you want to play a game?" I asked them.

"What sort of game?" Noah asked.

That had me stumped. I didn't know what kinds of games kids liked to play. Could a three-year-old play catch? I doubted it. I scanned the yard. I could make an obstacle course of some kind. We did that with horses in training sometimes.

"Follow me, I've got something fun in mind." I went to the

shed and grabbed a broom and shovel. I laid them about twenty feet apart.

"We're going to play a game of follow the leader. Are you ready?"

"Yeah."

"Yeah."

I placed my feet on either side of the broom and walked from one end to the other. They both copied. Then I ran at little legs pace to the shovel. They both ran beside me giggling away. I swear these had to be some of the happiest kids on earth. I jumped over the handle. Noah copied but Sarah was unsure. I offered her my hand which gave her the confidence she needed.

We ran to the swing set and circled it twice. Then I became a bridge and they had to crawl underneath me. We did some more running; in my mind I was hoping they were starting to fatigue. I became a mountain for them to climb over. Their energy seemed endless. But I started to see the subtle signs of tiredness–slower movements, less coordination.

Frankie and the twins were standing next to the broom watching us. "OK. Let's run to Aunty Frankie and we're done."

They took off, Sarah trailing her brother. I picked her up and ran with her making sure we matched Noah's pace. When we got there Frankie picked him up and spun him around.

"Let's go have morning tea," Frankie said.

I put the broom and shovel away before following them into the house. The four kids sat quietly in front of the TV. I went to help Frankie.

"Never thought I'd see a prince roll around in the dirt with some farm kids."

"Princes have many talents I'm sure you're not aware of."

"Such as?" She turned to face me; her body so close I could feel her breasts pressing against my chest.

"We like to roll around under the covers as well."

"Is that so?" Her breath brushed against my lips. Her body pushed against mine, sending electricity through me. I imagined her standing there in her lace bra and matching knickers. I wrapped one arm around her back pulling her tightly against me. The other cupped the back of her head, tangled in her pony tail. Her lips met mine and opened and I sought out her tongue. Her hands found their way around my back and held tight.

I couldn't let her go. I wouldn't. I'd wanted to kiss her like this for months. This was so much better than what I'd imagined. My erection pressed against her. I deepened the kiss, holding her tight. She sighed into my mouth.

I shouldn't have kissed her. I shouldn't have invited her down the road of misery I would soon be facing. Only one of us should have a broken heart.

CHAPTER TWENTY-EIGHT

Frankie

I DIDN'T WANT the kiss to stop. His lips were gentle but eager, but that tongue, it told me everything he wanted to do to me under those covers and I was more than willing. Our bodies were so close not an ounce of air would have fit between us. I couldn't tell if it was my heart beat thumping in my chest or his beating against mine. Heat spread through me and settled down below and turned into a yearning.

"Aunny Frannie, the soap won't come off."

I slowed the kiss but was unwilling to break it.

"Aunny Frannie."

The voice was closer. Our lips parted and I stared into Sebastian's eyes. His intense gaze made my heart do another thump. I turned to Sarah, who was holding her hands out to me. They were covered in a clear gel.

"What have you got on your hands?"

"Me and Noah washed them."

Noah came in next, holding his icky hands out. I backed away before he could touch me.

"Turn around. Do not touch anything. And go straight to the bathroom."

I hovered over them to make sure their hands didn't stray.

"We should really find out what they used," Sebastian said from behind me. "It could be dangerous."

"Noah, what's on your hands?"

"Soap."

"It's not soap. Show me what you used."

He didn't veer away from the bathroom. A tube sat on the vanity. A tube of lube.

Sebastian snapped his mouth closed and he regarded me slyly. He began washing the children's hands, with soap.

"It's not mine," I declared.

"It's not mine either."

"Uh-uh."

"It's not..."

I didn't think it would be. He wouldn't need it with me. All he did was kiss me and my knickers were wet. He hadn't even moved his hands while we kissed and my body had been captivated by him.

"Noah, where did you get this?"

"Uncle Brady's room."

"Oh God, that's gross." I picked up the tube and washed the gel off.

"Why's gross? Uncle Brady has his own soap."

"Yeah, Aunny Frannie, why's it gross?" Sebastian asked, grinning. I gave him the death stare. It never had the desired effect on him. I took the tube to Brady's room and shoved it under his pillow.

When I returned to the kitchen Sebastian was there. He shook his head. "They were alone for a few minutes."

I laughed.

CHAPTER TWENTY-NINE

Sebastian

We took our toasted sandwiches outside and had a picnic on the lawn. When we had finished, we all lay in the sun. The rays heated my face making me sleepy. I closed my eyes. Birds chirped in the trees. The children lay still and were quiet.

I relived the kiss with Frankie. I'd wanted to do that for as long as I could remember. The first time was probably the day she'd argued with me about how long it would take for her to get ready for the ball. I'd wanted to grab her and kiss her so hard she'd have no choice but to shut up.

A little body bumped into me. I opened my eyes and saw Noah peering at me. His eyebrows were furrowed. "Bastan."

"Yeah?"

"You kissed Aunny Frannie."

"Yeah."

"Dad will be happy," Tilly said.

"What?" Frankie and I said in unison.

"He said it was taking you forever."

I shook my head and held my laugh in. Were they all talking about us?

"It's good to keep Dad happy. You should kiss her more."

Oh, I had every intention of doing so. Frankie was unusually quiet. I turned my head to hers. She was smiling.

"Don't worry about keeping me happy, OK? My brother's the important one here," she said.

"I'm sure I can keep you both happy."

"I wasn't too impressed with the kiss."

"Is that so?"

She closed her eyes and gave a small shrug.

Noah shifted his weight and plopped himself into a sitting position on my stomach. I grunted as a whoosh of air escaped my lips.

"Follow the leader?" he asked.

"You want to play follow the leader?"

"Yes." He bounced.

I took hold of him and kept him still. "Why don't we have a rest first?"

"Play."

Sarah joined her brother and bounced up and down. I grunted with each bounce. And with each bounce their giggles got more exaggerated.

"Play. Play. Play," they chanted.

I sat up and sent them tumbling. They squealed in delight.

"Come on Aunty Frankie, follow the leader," I said.

She jumped up and put out her hands for the twins. She yanked them up, their feet leaving the ground, to their squealing delight. Frankie bent down in front of me, making a show of checking her laces and pushing her butt towards me. I gave it a soft slap on my way past. When she joined me at the start line, I whispered in her ear, "I'm not averse to putting on a show for the kids so they can report back to their dad."

"You're the leader," she said with a sly smile.

The kids had a never-ending stream of energy. At one point I thought they were nearly done but they got a second wind. When I thought I'd be stuck on the merry-go-round forever I heard Margaret call, "We're home."

CHAPTER THIRTY

**Frankie**

SEBASTIAN SIGHED and pushed the hair out of his face. I patted him on the back. "What do you think of big families now?"

"I think eight kids is probably the limit."

"I think eight foals would be better. Much easier."

He smiled. "At least you can leave them on their own. No tipped drawers. No lube."

"What's that about lube?" Mum asked, looking quizzically at Sebastian. Of course, that's the one thing she picked up on.

"The two little cherubs found a tube and decided to wash their hands with it," he said.

Before Mum could jump to any conclusions I said, "Best you ask Brady. They found it in his room."

She shook her head. "Did you have a good morning?"

"I couldn't find their off button," Sebastian said as Sarah

ran up to him and held her arms out to be picked up. Mum whisked her up instead, sparing him.

"Why don't we let Aunty Frankie and Uncle Sebastian have a rest before lunch?"

"OK."

Tilly ran over. "Nan, Sebastian kissed Aunty Frankie."

"Did he just?"

Was nothing sacred? I grabbed Sebastian's hand and pulled him away, out of earshot from Mum.

"Where are we going?"

"To bed."

"Oh yeah?" He wiggled his eyebrows.

"Really? Is that all you can think of?"

"A man could hope."

"I thought we could rest on the *sunbed* before lunch." I pointed to the simple wooden frame with wheels and a water-proof mattress on top.

"That doesn't sound nearly as exciting. But probably the better option. It would be creepy with your parents right here."

As I rearranged the pillows and hopped on, a message came up on his watch screen. He read it before dismissing it.

"You don't want to reply to your message?"

"Not now." He reached out for my hand. I shimmied closer to him eager to feel his touch. "It was my mother."

"You don't want to talk to her?"

"No. She'll want to know when I'm returning to Olean-der. That's all she ever wants."

"When are you going home?" I looked down at my hands not wanting to show how invested I was in his answer. On the inside the apprehension was like a lone radical cell bouncing around my chest.

He sighed and stared out into the garden. "I don't know… soon. I've been away for five years, minus some short visits. And it was uni and boarding school before that."

"I couldn't imagine not coming home," I said, staring out at the fields and the horses grazing.

"If this were my home, I wouldn't stay away."

Yet, I had. For my family. For my future.

"As soon as I set foot inside the castle, the expectation is that I'll stay there. No one asks how I am. No one asks how polo is. They just want to remind me of where I belong. But do I belong somewhere so oppressive?"

I held his hand tighter. It was impossible for me to imagine my life without my family. We loved and supported each other. No matter how long I was away, I was at peace the moment I drove back through the gates.

"But this decision is bigger than me or my heart. What would it say to Oleander if I chose not to return and lead them? Would they think they have no need for a royal family? That it's irrelevant?"

He tugged at his collar. When he turned his face to mine, I could see the anguish. Would my parents ever ask me to do something that made me so unhappy? But like he said, it wasn't just about him. They needed to consider an entire nation.

I didn't have an answer for him. I couldn't leave the home I loved. How could he return to a home he didn't?

"Tell me some good things about Oleander." I snuggled closer to him. I watched his face as he spoke.

"It's always green. Spring and summer are the best

seasons because it's warm. The sun brings out the flowers, and deciduous trees get new growth. It smells glorious." He gave a small smile.

"That sounds nice. Are there many horses there?"

"Yes. I want to set up a retraining and rehoming program for retired polo horses from across Europe. I'd love to work with the horses to help them find a better future."

I bit my lip. That's what he must have been speaking to my dad about at the polo stables. His dream property. Dad had never mentioned Sebastian's dreams mirrored my own. Was this another part of their conniving plot? Like bringing him here was a ploy to bring us closer.

"Just like what I want to do here."

"Yes, but mine is just a dream. My parents have said they won't support me."

My head snapped up. "What do you mean they won't support you?"

"They think my sole role is to run the country not 'play with four-legged animals'. Their words, not mine."

"But surely having a leader who shows empathy to animals is something to be celebrated."

"Having empathy for the animals and actively working with them are two different things. I don't know. I mean, why should they have a say in what I do? I'm an adult."

He shrugged and rested back against the pillows.

"I don't know if I could ever allow someone to have that much control over my life."

"They lost most of their control when they sent me to boarding school. They thought it would teach me discipline and help guide me to be a better leader. It did those things but not in the way they wanted."

He sighed and I rubbed his hand in response.

"Now I think about what it would be like if I went back. I haven't lived there full time in fifteen years. I've been playing professional polo for the last five."

"What do you think it would be like if you go back?"

I wasn't sure if I wanted to know the answer.

"I would never have the freedom I do now. As soon as I stepped out of the castle grounds the media would be there. I'd have to interact with people who are only interested in me because of my title."

I tried to imagine what it would be like living like that. I'd rather be in shorts and a singlet than dressed in some stuffy outfit. Imagine the horror if they saw my shorts and boots tan. And then having to worry about every little thing I did and said, it sounded like a nightmare.

"You're lucky, Frankie. Don't you ever forget that. Your family love you for you. They accept everything about you, embrace it even."

He took my hand and kissed it. I leant over and cupped his face. I pressed my lips against his. I wanted him to know he wasn't alone in this world. That I liked him for him.

CHAPTER THIRTY-ONE

Sebastian

WE SAT around the lunch table. The kids were telling Billy and Louise all about their morning. They gave Billy detailed instructions on how to play follow the leader.

When they'd finished their in-depth instructions, Jim said, "We're going out mustering tomorrow. There's rain due in a few days so we want to get the herd in before that, before they calve."

"Do you think you're up for a big ride polo boy? Or should I call you the kissing prince?" Billy said.

"I think I can handle it."

"Hours in the saddle?"

"There's nothing I'd enjoy more."

"Are you sure about that?" He gave me a wry smile.

I shook my head. I needed to stop falling for his traps. He was so witty he always had a comeback ready. "How far will we be going?"

"We need to go out to the forestry, around twenty kilometres away," Jim said.

"The place where you agist that you spoke about yesterday?"

"Yeah." Billy nodded.

"How are we going to find the cows?"

"We know the general location because we check on them regularly," Jim explained. We put out mineral lick and molasses. They've learnt what the ute and truck sound like."

"So, when they hear us, they come," Billy said.

"Why can't you take the truck out to get them?" Frankie asked from beside me.

"We got a load in last week but we couldn't fit them all," Jim said, passing the warm bread rolls to Louise. "Some are too pregnant to be trucked."

"If they're so pregnant why did you leave it until now to bring them in?" Frankie asked.

"The majority of the herd aren't due for another few weeks. I suspect the neighbour's bull got to these cows."

She nodded and passed the rolls to me. I grabbed one.

"Do you want one?" I asked Noah who was sitting on my other side.

He nodded, his action so eager I smiled. "Bastan, can you butter it for me please?"

"Sure." I tore the roll open and waited for the butter to reach us.

"I like the butter all over."

I followed his explicit instruction and made sure I covered every white part in butter. I showed it to him. "Like this?"

"Yes," he said, giving me a big smile.

Frankie leant over and whispered in my ear, "You're the first person to ever get it right."

I felt proud. Yes, the Crown Prince of Oleander was proud that he could butter a roll perfectly in the eyes of a four-year-old.

———

"DID YOU BRING RIDING BOOTS?" Frankie called from her room.

"Of course."

"What sort of boots?" Scepticism filled her voice.

"I brought some RM Williams boots."

"Of course you did," she said from the doorway.

"What's that supposed to mean?"

"Well, only a rich person would buy $500 boots for a week or two in the country."

"I'll have you know that I love these boots. I've had them for months. I've worn them before this trip and I'll wear them after."

She sat on my bed and offered me a small smile. "Sorry, that was rude of me. You'll need a warm jumper or jacket. It's quite cool riding early in the morning."

"OK." I sat beside her. "Is it hard to muster?"

"Not really. It will be easier if they're nearly ready to calve. They will want to stay together. As long as we point them in the right direction, we should be OK."

"Did you muster a lot growing up?"

"Yep. Living on a farm you need to be involved with everything."

We lay on the bed together and spoke for hours about

horses, farm life and her family. When Frankie fell asleep fully clothed minus her boots beside me, I didn't have the heart to wake her. I got the quilt off her bed to cover us.

When she rolled into me, I didn't feel guilty about enjoying her touch. Not seeing that I finally had hope. But I did feel guilty about that: having hope that she'd fallen for me like I'd fallen for her. I tried to tell myself I wasn't leading her on. I'd always been open about returning to Oleander, but I should have stopped these feelings before they'd even started. Especially since my homecoming was overdue.

CHAPTER THIRTY-TWO

Frankie

"We'll meet you out there," Dad said. "We'll have the cows yarded and ready to go."

"OK."

We mounted and headed for the gate of the long paddock. We rode along in silence. I smiled to myself. Sebastian was just like me, liking to warm up to the day before we started conversing with the world.

There was a slight breeze that rustled the grass. The backwards and forward sway of my body as Jane moved beneath me was relaxing. She was named Jane because she was all brown with no markings – Plain Jane. But what she missed out on in colour she made up for in smarts, speed and personality. I had broken her in myself with dad's guidance, and we'd put miles on her together when we went riding out in the forestry to check on the cows.

Trees dotted the paddock here and there; our ancestors having cleared the land over a century ago. Dad had been replanting over the last few years, trying to create a wildlife corridor.

"This is the traditional country of the Wakka Wakka people," I said as we walked along. "They would say Yhurri Gurri."

"What does that mean?"

"It means, 'Come this way, welcome friend'."

Sebastian smiled.

"It's nice to be walking in the Git'ti Jigamba: in the sun time."

"Are the Wakka Wakka still here?"

"There are some ancestors still here. They were pushed off their land by pastoralists nearly two hundred years ago," Frankie said.

"What happened to them?"

"It was violent. People on both sides died. The Wakka Wakka were pushed further west. Some lived and worked on stations while some were relocated to Fraser Island. They were scattered and most lost their language and culture."

I hated thinking about it. I imagined how I would feel if they forcibly removed me.

"In the early 1900s a reserve was built and some Wakka Wakka went there. The conditions were terrible and the food rations were a disgrace. They were sent out to work and had to clear the land which was once theirs."

I shuddered thinking about it. All of it. Many people thought this was Gubbi Gubbi land. But unlike white people borders, Aboriginal borders were not succinct, they were more fluid. We'd met the ancestors of the land and they told us how the Wakka Wakka managed their country completely different to white people. They had a close relationship and respect for all living things. They didn't hunt to excess, they understood seasons according to what was flowering, they could read signs in nature and they didn't clear land as they respected how all living things evolved and relied on each other. We should have learnt from them instead of turning them away.

"Indigenous people across the world suffered the same indignity," Sebastian said. He shook his head. "It's all about power and money."

"It's sad to think about. They lost their identity. They were forbidden to speak their language so a lot of it was lost. They are trying to regain all that knowledge now. They've written dictionaries and they teach children at school."

Kangaroos sat up in the grass and watched as we rode past. I pointed them out to Sebastian. "Look at the guroman in the ban."

"Wow," he said as he surveyed the scenery. "The more I look for them the more I see."

"They're everywhere. If they hit plague proportions, we request a permit to cull. If we didn't, our paddocks would be bare and our animals would have nothing to eat."

When we passed them, they put their heads down and resumed eating.

"It's amazing out here. So quiet. Almost like we're the only people in the world," Sebastian said.

"I love it. It's not just the outward peace, it settles on the inside too."

"If we had horses on the estate, I would likely ride for hours."

I swung my head in his direction.

"You don't have horses at the castle? The Queen of England has horses. She's over ninety and still rides."

"Nope. No horses."

"If you become king, you can do whatever you want. You could have as many horses as you want."

"Yeah." His jaw clenched and he looked away. I'd tried to make him feel better but had somehow made it worse. It could be a long time until he became king. His mother could live for another forty years. If he went home, it could mean no horses for forty years.

We got to the fence line. When we reached the gate, I swung Jane's back end so I could reach the latch, then bent to open it. When we went through, I reversed the process. We left the sparse trees behind us and bush took over. We needed to ride single file through most parts. The shade from the trees made it cooler. Sunlight filtered through, leaving dappled patterns of light and shade on the ground and shrubbery. The light moved as the breeze stirred the branches above us. The constant rustling of leaves mixed with the bird songs. Lyrical magpies harmonized with whistles and chirps.

I breathed in the freshness, letting it settle deep in my lungs. Looking at one of the tall gums on my right I saw a goanna hugging the trunk. Its dark skin stood out against the grey bark. Its wide splayed claws dug in to keep it attached. I stopped so I could show Sebastian. Turning in my saddle I pointed to the goanna. Sebastian's eyes widened. "What's that?"

"A goanna. I'd estimate it's about a metre and a half in length."

"It's beautiful."

It sure was. Its entire body formed a wavy line from its long neck to its spotted thick torso to its stripy elongated tail.

"Are they dangerous?"

"Their claws and teeth can do some damage. And I wouldn't want to get in the way of that tail. It could easily knock a child over."

"Are they aggressive?"

"They rarely attack unless provoked. Sometimes, if they're scared and trying to escape, they might think a person is a tree and climb it." I shuddered, thinking about the claws digging in.

When we got to the cattle yards, Dad and Billy were waiting for us with morning tea of scones and juice spread out on the bonnet of the car. I led Sebastian to the creek before dismounting. I enjoyed his company, whether we were talking or riding in silence. Nothing was forced with him.

"Let the horses drink and rest while we eat," I said.

We headed back to the ute.

"How's the royal butt coping?" Billy asked.

"You do know he rides for a living, right?" I said

"But usually not for four hours straight."

"Maybe not, but polo is more intense than just sitting in a saddle," I pointed out.

"Ooh, look at my little sis, sticking up for her royal lover boy," Billy said.

I gave him the finger and scarfed down a scone.

Dad looked toward the yarded cows. "Some of these cows look like they're close to calving. They have pretty big bags and a couple have teets that are filling."

"That means we may not make it home before one drops," I said to Sebastian.

"Drops?"

"Gives birth."

Sebastian nodded.

"And the rain looks like it's closing in too," Dad said.

Sebastian peered up at the sky. There was nothing but blue sky above us. He looked at me.

"Dad would have listened to the local ABC radio station and watched the radar."

Sebastian blushed. "That makes sense."

"We've got your swags in the back and Mum has packed you lunch. You may want to save some in case you need to stay overnight," Dad said.

"That could be romantic," Billy said.

"I'm sure it could be, especially if you're not there," Sebastian fired back.

CHAPTER THIRTY-THREE

Sebastian

LEAVING HER FAMILY BEHIND, we set off for the farm with Frankie leading, the cows behind her and me in the rear. The horses ambled keeping pace with the cows. My job was to alert Frankie to any strange behaviour and to let her know if a cow strayed. I had no idea what I was looking for and hoped I'd recognise it when I saw it.

The cows walked at a steady pace letting out a moo every now and then. They all appeared happy to just follow along. The ground beneath was dirt, and sporadic clumps of grass cushioned their feet and silenced any sound of their footfalls.

Frankie turned in her saddle. When she caught my eye, she smiled. I felt light in the saddle like her smile lifted my whole being.

After about three hours Frankie stopped the herd near a creek.

"We're about half way," she said as she dismounted. She took Jane's bridle off and hung it on a branch. I followed suit.

Then she pulled her swag off her back. "It makes a comfortable seat."

We sat next to each other on the rolled-up swag and shared lunch. The cows stayed close, picking at the grass. One of them stood apart from the others.

"Lucky we stopped when we did," Frankie said.

The cow lay down, her head flat to the ground. After a few minutes she stood again. She walked around for a few minutes and laid down again. I kept a close eye on my watch and the cow. Her behaviour continued for ninety minutes. Frankie and I untacked the horses. We wouldn't be going home today. I watched as Frankie undid the compression straps and rolled out my swag.

"It's just like a tent but only big enough for one person, unless it's king size like mine."

I watched as she connected the poles and the inserted them through the fabric sleeves and connected them to the pins on each corner. She clicked the poles into the clips. The longest pole went at the head of the swag and the shortest at the foot. Both ends flopped into the centre. How was one supposed to sleep in that? I couldn't imagine how it was going to stay up. She pulled on a guy rope at the head end so the swag stood up rigid and pegged it into the ground. Then did the same with the foot end. It looked like a half cylinder. She unzipped it and peered inside. I joined her.

"On the bottom is a thin mattress so you're not lying on the hard ground. There's a sleeping bag in here for you too." I peeked into the swag and saw the sleeping bag laid out on the mattress. "If it's a warm night, you can unzip the top flap of canvas so there would be just mesh between you and the night."

"OK." It was certainly a level closer to nature than I was accustomed to, but was excited to experience.

"Probably not tonight though, if that rain is coming."

She put her swag up, about two metres away. I didn't understand the need for such distance until she said, "Can you help me find a log to roll over for us to sit on? Then we need to collect some firewood so we can build a fire between the swags."

"Won't a fire be dangerous?" I scanned area, noting the brittle, dry grass.

"By the time we go to sleep it will just be embers. It will be perfectly safe."

As we were putting some dried branches on the wood pile, Frankie stood up and grabbed my hand. "Sebastian look."

The cow was lying on her side. The start of the sack was coming out of the vulva as the cow's body was contracting. When the contractions hit, her whole rear end would lift and the calf would come out a little more.

The sack broke and the calf's front legs poked through. The cow hardly made a sound, even through the great contractions causing her body to swell and subside. The calf kept coming an inch at a time. Its head appeared next. I held my breath when the suction after a push led to the calf being pulled in a couple of inches. I must have sucked in my breath in response. Frankie gave my hand a reassuring squeeze.

It was amazing how the cow held her tail up and out of the way the entire time. With one last push the calf was out and the cow stood up to lick the mucous off her baby. It was like she hadn't just given birth. The calf was not moving.

"It's not breathing," Frankie said. "Its chest isn't rising."

She let go of my hand and made her way to the calf. "I'll

clear the mucous out of its mouth and nose. Then I need you to rub the calf's side and chest with your hands."

The mucous-covered calf lay below us, and its mum watched us with caution. We stayed on the opposite side of the calf.

"It's alright, Mumma...good girl...we're just here to help," Frankie said in a soothing tone. She opened the calf's mouth and stuck her fingers in. In a sweeping motion she pulled the mucous out. She did the same with the nose.

When she had finished, I knelt on one knee and rubbed the calf's side with vigour while Frankie spoke to the cow. The calf was motionless beneath my hands. Even though my arms tired, panic kept me going. I changed the direction of my hands, glancing at Frankie for reassurance. She nodded her approval. The calf gave a small jerk and then a grunt. I slowed down the rubbing as its chest rose and fell beneath my hands. I took in a rattling breath, too, then sighed with relief.

When I stood back, Frankie took my slimy hand in hers and gave me a kiss. We left the mother and baby to resume their cleaning routine and washed our hands in the creek.

"What are you smiling at?" Frankie asked.

CHAPTER THIRTY-FOUR

Frankie

WHEN SEBASTIAN TURNED his smile on me my heart did a leap. "I just watched the most amazing thing with my favourite person in the world, why wouldn't I be smiling?"

My heart beat faster as he stepped towards me, and I realised he'd called me his favourite person. His muscular arms wrapped around my waist and pulled me towards him. My arms looped around his neck as if they knew that's where they belonged. Our mouths found each other and opened. He tasted as good as the chocolate brownies we'd had for lunch, and I wanted to get closer. I wanted to climb him like a goanna. I had to suppress my giggle at the thought.

His hands moved. One to my lower back pulling me even closer and the other between my shoulder blades trapping me in the kiss I had no intention of leaving, anyway.

As my body heated up for him the breeze picked up and the temperature around us fell. The rustling of the trees became a steadier beat.

The rain.

I ripped my lips away. "Take your clothes off."

Sebastian's wide eyes stared at me. "What?"

I pushed myself away from him. We didn't have long.

"Listen." I waited for him to look like he was paying attention. "The rain is close. Take your clothes off and put them in your swag."

I didn't wait for him to answer. I stripped down to my bra and underwear and threw my clothes into his swag.

"If we get wet in our clothes, we'll freeze all night."

Sebastian followed my lead.

"Get the saddle pads and saddles and put them in there too. Otherwise we'll be oiling them for the next week."

The rain freight train was thundering closer. I ran to check on the horses. Their heads were up, listening, but they didn't appear frightened. The cow and calf were huddling together. Poor bubba, imagine being greeted by this rain on your first day in the world. I turned. Sebastian was waiting near the swags. My steps faltered as I took the sight in. The only material covering his tantalising body was his underwear. And that did little to disguise his package. I suddenly realised how little I was wearing, with my boyleg undies and sports bra. Not the sexiest thing in the world.

I stood and watched as his eyes roved my body. His legs were well muscled, waist slim and shoulders broad. His t-shirt tan matched mine.

The rain was nearly upon us. The first few drops hit my skin. I ran to him, grabbed his hand and pulled him to my swag. I pushed him in. The rain was in our tiny clearing. I climbed in after Sebastian. As I sat beside him and reached for the zip, my fingers fumbled. Rain drops started hitting the swag. I grabbed the zip and pulled it. The canvas closed around us as the rain pelted the swag.

Our bodies were so close, so bare, the space heated in no time. I lay beside Sebastian. No sooner had my back hit the mattress than his lips met mine. His hand found my breast. Damn bra was in the way. I lifted myself up so I could undo the clasp and tear it off. His lips and hand were back instantly.

My moan was drowned out by the rain. I wrapped my leg around him in an attempt to get closer. My back hit the cold canvas of the swag, making me shiver. I moved in closer to him. His lips drew away and he said my name. I yanked him back down. It was not the time for talking.

I changed position so I could manoeuvre my underwear off, without breaking contact with his lips. It was a contortion act in such close quarters. I was desperate to not lose contact, adding to the difficulty. Sebastian raised himself up so our lips disconnected. He was breathing heavy.

He pulled his underwear off. The swag shook as he banged into the side of it. I raised myself up to meet his lips again. His hands moved from breast to breast, and each nipple went hard. Heat followed his hand as it moved down my side stopping at my hip. My stomach did that Sebastian lurch. His mere touch ignited a passion in me I never knew existed. Our kiss deepened. Hardness pressed against me. His hand reached between my legs and I opened them wider, begging for him. His fingers slid in easily.

"You're so wet."

"For you."

That's all the invitation he needed. He rolled on top of me

and pushed himself in. Nothing could have prepared me for how good it felt. He sank in further as my legs widened, my knee brushed the side of the swag but I didn't care about the coolness anymore. Our harsh breaths could hardly be heard above the rain.

He slowed his pace and lowered his head next to mine.

"I never thought I'd have sex with a prince in a swag."

His lips moved towards mine. Before he claimed them, he said, "It won't be the last time either."

Each time he slid out he hit the magic spot. I clutched the side of the mattress. His long body was heavy against mine but light at the same time. Each stroke made me feel closer to him, like our body and souls had become entwined. I thanked him silently when his lips drew away; I couldn't concentrate on kissing him anymore. With his mouth so close to my ear his heavy breathing and grunts mixed with moans were loud, almost like they were pressing down on me. I didn't think it was possible to be turned on any more than I already was. That did it.

With each thrust my body wanted more. I wanted more. I wrapped my arms around his back and clenched his shoulders. He thrusted faster. I came closer to the ledge. I arched my back so he not only hit the spot sliding out but in as well. I held tighter. I was close. So close.

"Come for me, Frankie."

On his demand my entire body opened up to him like the current sucking a wave out, and I clenched around his dick trying to take him with me. He kept his pace. I gripped his shoulders as my whole body spasmed, his weight holding me there as I cried out. He thrust again and again moaning as he emptied himself inside me. When he lay on top of me, his dick jerked in its one last effort.

Our hot sweaty bodies held each other close.

CHAPTER THIRTY-FIVE

Sebastian

"Sebastian." Frankie's soft voice filled the swag. Our bodies were still entwined, her head on my shoulder and her leg over mine. "Sebastian, you need to get up."

"You want more sex?" I asked still half asleep.

"Sebastian." Her whisper was more urgent. "My brother's here."

I jerked up so quickly that I hit my head on the top of the swag and Frankie flopped onto the mattress. Her brother? Here? We were both half naked—or three-quarters naked...or mostly naked.

"But...our clothes are in the other swag," I said to her. I stared in the direction of my swag as if I could see through the canvas and measure the distance. Too far. Why hadn't I been summoned at twelve to go to Hogwarts? Magic powers would have served me well at that moment.

"I know that."

I didn't move. I could think of nothing more awkward

than stepping out of the swag in nothing but my underwear to face Billy. He'd know straight away what we had been doing. No, wait, her dad standing there would have been worse.

"You'll have to go get them," she said.

There was no choice. I couldn't expect her to do it. I reached behind me to retrieve her bra. She raised herself to put it on while I considered how to approach this. Just like ripping a Band-Aid off would be the best solution, I opened the zip and sprang out into the morning sunlight. I stretched to the sky; my movement exaggerated.

I stared at the man standing in front of my swag. I froze.

It wasn't Billy.

Tall, with the same brown hair as Billy's, but his was cut close.

He crossed his arms and looked me up and down.

"Well, well, well. Dare I ask what you've been doing with my little sister?"

His biceps bulged from his shirt as he pushed his chest out. His hard stare was nearly as impressive as Frankie's.

"Hi...I'm um...Sebastian."

"Brady." He continued to stare. Was this a family trait or something? Would I have to endure this from our children?

"Your stare isn't nearly as impressive as Frankie's."

He roared with laughter, just the same as his dad's. "Billy said I would like you."

He strode over and shook my hand. Like shaking the hand of a man standing there in his underwear was the most normal thing to do. "Get yourself dressed. I'll get the horses."

And just like that the most awkward family introduction was over.

"Great to have you home, Frankie. I must say the first man you've ever brought home is a winner."

We got dressed and tacked up the horses.

"I'll take the lead and you two can follow behind," Brady said.

"The calf is too young to walk," Frankie said.

"The calf is too young for many things but that didn't stop you two from educating it last night."

Great, another smart arse in the family.

"Yeah, well, at least I didn't corrupt my three- and four-year-old niece and nephew with my lube."

"If you two weren't so busy kissing they wouldn't have found my lube."

"If you liked girls instead of boys you wouldn't need lube."

They went back and forth like this while they collected the calf and slung it across Brady's horse, in front of the saddle.

The revelation that Brady was gay and accepted by all the family made me love them all the more. Before Frankie mounted her horse, I pulled her towards me and kissed her. I wanted that kiss to convey everything I felt for her. How every part of me loved her and wanted to stay with her.

We rode side by side. Sometimes talking, sometimes in silence. Just looking at her I knew this was where I belonged. This place was where her heart was. And where hers was, so was mine.

"What are you smiling at?" Frankie asked.

"I was just thinking about how happy you look. That I understand now why you think you belong here. You do. It's a part of you."

She glanced away but quickly looked back. "I'm happy because of you, too."

"You could be happy here without me, though."

"Just because I could, it doesn't mean I want to."

What was I going to say, that I wanted to stay with her on the farm, to share our dream together? I couldn't say that. I couldn't give her hope where hope didn't exist. I would be gone soon.

Soon. That was being deliberately vague. Especially when I knew *soon* was less than two weeks away. Rather than share what I truly wanted, I said, "I'd rather stay with you, here. But I can't make a promise I have to break."

"I know." She reached for my hand and gave it a squeeze.

CHAPTER THIRTY-SIX

Frankie

SEBASTIAN and I did the dishes together after lunch as if it were our routine. He was a prince but never had any qualms about doing mundane chores. Since we'd arrived home, the only time I'd really thought about him being a prince was when I thought about the prospect of him leaving. He'd been a part of my life for so many months; it would be weird without him.

Without him. My heart clenched.

"We should go out and work with the horses. We haven't spent much time with them yet," I said as I put a plate in the drainer.

"What do you want to start with?"

"We need to start handling them so they become more confident with us."

"That's a good idea." He put the glasses he'd dried away. "I think the gelding will come around. He always looks like he wants to join in but he's that tiny bit too scared."

We went into the paddock with lead ropes and halters, some brushes and training sticks. We didn't plan to use them all unless the horses were ready. But having them with us meant the horses could see the items and learn they were nothing to fear. We walked half way to the horses and waited for them to come the rest of the way. It showed both trust and respect when they did.

"Have you worked with horses like this before?" I asked Sebastian.

"No. When I trained with Juan's dad or at the polo stables the horses had already been handled and had ground training."

I approached the horses. "I don't want them to feel pressured or threatened so I don't look at them directly."

Sebastian watched and did the same. We each chose a mare to pat. I extended my pats across the body and down the legs, and I changed the pressure I applied as I went.

"They all need a farrier but we need to make sure they are well handled first."

Sebastian nodded. "And they need to be able to be held."

"That will be the next step. Before we finish today, we will walk around them with the halter and lead. That's it, the first lesson will be done. They just need to see that it's nothing to be scared of."

I finished patting the mare and moved towards the gelding. He stepped away. He wasn't tready yet, and I wasn't going to force him. I went to the other mare instead. When Sebastian finished, he stood a metre away from the gelding and watched me. We talked as my hands made their way around the mare.

I glanced at Sebastian. The gelding had come closer to

him. Sebastian turned his body so he was more open to the gelding while telling him he was a good boy. The gelding did not run; he stood and watched Sebastian's movements.

I continued to make my way around the mare. Sebastian had turned in full towards the gelding. He didn't make eye contact or stick his hand out, even though he was in touching distance. The gelding came another step closer. His body contradicted his head: one leant back while the other pressed forward to smell Sebastian.

I picked up the lead rope and walked around all the mares before giving them a final pat. Sebastian was still talking with the gelding. He lifted his palm up but made no attempt to pat the horse.

I should have known Sebastian would be perfect for this. He was gentle and calm. I didn't want to do this without him. I wanted him by my side to share the joy, to learn with, to learn from. I didn't want to live my dream alone. Oh God, I'd fallen in love with a person I couldn't have. Could I be any more stupid?

I shook my head.

Up till that moment, I had been happy to be by myself. But Sebastian had changed that. He never pushed me into anything. He never forced my decision. He was just himself.

I didn't know whether to tell him. But what would be the point? He didn't want to leave, although he knew he had to, and this would only make it harder for him. That wouldn't be fair.

As the gelding walked off Sebastian turned to me and smiled. My heart nearly burst out of my chest.

CHAPTER THIRTY-SEVEN

Sebastian

Frankie was staring at me.

"I think that went well." My words broke her out of her trance. She bent down to collect the gear we'd brought into the paddock.

"Yes, I think so."

I expected her to tell me how we would progress tomorrow, but that's all she said.

I followed her to the gate and opened it for her. She didn't say thank you like she normally would. She avoided making eye contact with me.

"Let's take their afternoon hay out to them." She walked ahead of me, not beside me, and went to the mother horse first before heading to the big paddock.

"What are you thinking about?"

She opened her mouth and closed it again. After dropping her biscuits of hay, she turned to me. "You're a natural with horses. I...when you..." She took a deep breath. "I don't think you should give up your dream of working with horses. I know you say your parents won't support you. But you could still do it."

Maybe I could. Her belief in me made me stronger.

Messages had been coming through my phone all morning. As we made our way back to the house, I checked them. Every single one of them was from my mother.

Sebastian, The polo season in Australia ended two weeks ago. It's time for your return.

Sebastian, I have tried to contact your bodyguards. It goes straight through to voicemail. If this is a deliberate attempt to avoid me, I do not appreciate it.

I am getting impatient with your evasive behaviour. Call me.

It would do me no good to evade her any longer. If she became riled up enough, she would send an investigator to find me. My visit with Frankie's family was only intended to be two weeks. But in those first few days I had grown closer to each of them. I found a place I believed would bring me happiness. But those messages from my mother had deflated any hope. In fact, it was reckless of me to have any hope in the first place.

I needed to address this situation.

CHAPTER THIRTY-EIGHT

Frankie

WE TOOK the horses into the round yard one by one and worked with them. We wanted them to respond to our body language and move their feet to our cues.

Then it was the gelding's turn. Sebastian approached him in the paddock with the halter and lead rope. Just like he had the day before, he patted the gelding while holding them. Then he rubbed the gelding all over with the supplies. The gelding accepted it all and didn't flinch. Sebastian then did the same thing with the training stick.

The twins and I watched as Sebastian tied the rope around the gelding's neck and pulled on it to apply pressure. This way the gelding knew he was caught. Sebastian slipped the halter on. Again, the gelding showed nothing but trust. Sebastian untied the knot in the lead rope and led the gelding to the round yard. The horse soon learnt to come off the pressure. He walked without needing to be pulled. He was obliging and willing, always trying to please.

Once in the round yard, Sebastian let the gelding go. He stood and watched Sebastian. Sebastian took a step towards him, his body pointing towards the horse's shoulder and the stick pointing to his bum. He moved closer towards him and the gelding started walking around the outside.

"We want to try to get three paces today," I said. "Walk, trot and canter. Then change direction and do the same."

Sebastian and the gelding were in tune with each other. Sebastian applied pressure slowly and clucked when he wanted a change in pace. I was surprised that he was able to keep the gelding's feet moving the whole time. When Sebastian stopped moving so did the gelding. Once again, another perfect job.

But perfection didn't always last forever. We were only a temporary part of Sebastian's life. His destiny awaited him in his homeland. Soon the horses would become another memory for Sebastian. Like me.

"Are you alright?" Sebastian asked, breaking into my thoughts.

"Never better." I grabbed the equipment and held it tight, as if I were creating a shield around myself and my heart. Too late. It would need more than a shield to protect it now.

CHAPTER THIRTY-NINE

Sebastian

We stood and surveyed the charming two-storey brown brick and cement rendered building known as The Story Bank. It was a square box but the arched windows, recessed porch and classical influences made it a building of beauty.

"This was an old bank building," Frankie explained. "The bank was downstairs and the living quarters upstairs. That is where P.L. Travers, the author of *Mary Poppins* was born."

"Come on, Uncle Sebastian," Tilly and Livvy said as they each took a hand and dragged me to the entrance. We paid our fee, entered the building and were greeted just inside the door by a staircase. Sliding down the banister were sculptures of Jane and Michael, from *Mary Poppins*.

"Isn't it cool, Uncle Sebastian?"

"We tried to slide down the banisters at home once. Mum was not happy. She thought we'd fall and crack our skull open."

Frankie laughed. "To be fair. If your brother and sister

saw you and copied, they would likely fall and crack their skulls open."

"I suppose."

An insistent ringing came from the room on the left. When we entered the study, I saw the sound was coming from an old-time phone on the desk, one with an actual dial for the numbers. It rang and rang until I picked it up to answer it.

In the poshest voice I could muster I said, "Hello, Sebastian here."

The girls giggled.

"Please bring the horse and carriage around at a quarter to the hour." No response. I hung up.

Frankie handed me a map and a pencil. "There are twenty mice painted in various places around the building. Good luck finding them."

Tilly led me to a screen. "These are Story Bank Tellers. There are five of them. You write a part of the story into each one and then at the end you can print it out."

I read the info. The first prompt was about treasured places and possessions. "Do you want me to write a story?" I asked the twins.

Tilly and Livvy nodded in unison. I started typing making sure no one was watching.

Once upon a time there was a prince. He visited a place called Australia. Beauty was everywhere, nature abounded and bird songs welcomed every day. It was a treasured place with a short but interesting history. He loved it and the people so much he never wanted to leave.

"What are you writing?" Tilly asked, standing on her tiptoes, straining to see over my shoulder.

"It's a secret." I saved what I had written and turned to her. "Where to next?"

"In here." She took my hand and led me through a wide doorway.

"What room is this?"

"It's called the character room," Livvy recited as if she'd been here a dozen times, "and it has a Cabinet of Curiosities."

There was so much to look at I didn't know where to start. The wooden cabinet stood taller than me and took up two metres of floor space. There were doors and drawers to pull out hiding little treasures like a pocket watch and letters. Another story bank screen was there, this one asking who the characters were.

The prince met a fair lady there. Her name was Frankie. She was as beautiful as beautiful can be. When she laughed the entire world lit up. Prince Sebastian fell in love with her. But the fair lady denied him for many months.

Livvy tried to look around me as I wrote. When I glanced at her, she gave me a cheeky smile. I gave her a little tap away.

"Don't forget the mice," Tilly prompted me. Lucky she had. I had forgotten. I went to the next Story Bank Teller.

Prince Sebastian visited her home. That's when he fell in love with her family as well. They were just like Frankie – full of life and love. They teased each other and made jokes. They ate together and talked about their day. Each and every one of them cared for the others. Laughter filled their home and it was unlike anything he had ever experienced.

The library came next with its dark wooden book cases and heavy maroon curtains. I could see myself lounging on the chaise reading one of the many books. Another Story Bank teller stood in the corner, asking me to tell it more about my characters. While Frankie explored the Cabinet of Curiosities with Tilly and Livvy, I wrote from the heart.

With all of his being he wanted to stay with that family. He had never felt so much love as he had in those days he spent there. And the fair lady gave him understanding and a strength he never expected.

"This place is amazing," I said to Frankie as I left the library. "Whoever came up with these ideas is smart. It's not only good for kids but adults as well."

The twins grabbed my hand to take me to the next room. On the way they stopped under a plastic arbour of cherry trees. Tilly went and grabbed Frankie and set us both up under the cherry tree. Then she asked for my phone to take photos.

"Pretend you're in love," she said to us, readying the camera.

"That won't be hard." I pulled Frankie towards me. "I love you, Frankie."

Frankie froze and stared at me, a dazed look on her face. My heart raced. I pulled her towards me and kissed her there under those trees and kissed her again. Then I twirled her around and dipped her. Frankie laughed. Livvy clapped. When I straightened up, I saw we had an audience. I turned and skipped down the cherry tree lane.

"What a lovely family," an elderly lady said behind us.

We walked through the house, enjoying all that there was to see. Every room was themed after a snippet of the Mary Poppins story. We all joined in the fun in the Shadow Theatre where we played with the shapes of ladies, dragons, castles and carriages making up stories of our own until the dragons ate the ladies.

Happily ever after seemed impossible. But he would do everything he could to find a way. And it seemed possible now because Frankie showed him who he could become.

"Can we read the story, Uncle Sebastian?"

"Not today. It's for Aunty Frankie."

But I wouldn't give it to her yet. Not until the day I had to leave.

My heart was in my throat. I had just told her I loved her and all along I knew I had to leave. Why did I do that?

"AUNTY FRANKIE, who's that with Pop?" Tilly asked as we parked in front of the house.

"It's Amanda and Juan." Frankie smiled broadly and waved to them.

The girls ran ahead and wrapped Jim in a hug.

"Did you have fun?"

"It was great. Uncle Sebastian found all of the mice."

"He had to go around twice because he missed some the first time."

"And he played with us in the Shadow Theatre."

The Uncle Sebastian comment hadn't gone unnoticed: Amanda and Juan gave each other a wry smile.

"Jim showed us your new horses," Amanda said looking towards the paddock.

"Frankie and Sebastian have been working with them just about every day," Jim said. "The horses have come such a long way already. At first, they didn't want to come near us. Now, they come straight up to us when we enter the paddock."

"You've managed that in less than a week?" Amanda asked.

Frankie grabbed my hand. The movement caught the attention of the other pair.

"The gelding was the most timid. Sebastian has been working with him twice a day."

Dad took hold of the twins' hands. "I'll leave you to it. Come on, girls."

Frankie led us over to the paddock. She couldn't stop smiling as she spoke about the horses.

"The mare looking at us. She's the bravest one," she said.

"The first few days we were here we just fed them and tried to get them acquainted with us," I said.

"And then we started working with them—"

"It's been four days now and we have achieved so much."

Frankie nodded. "The gelding was very timid to start with—"

"But he just needed time."

"Sebastian has been great with him, always patient. They really connected." Frankie gave me a smile.

"Stop," Amanda said abruptly.

We stopped and looked at her.

She gestured between us. "How long has this been a thing?"

"What thing?" Frankie asked, crossing her arms.

Juan looked at Amanda as if Frankie were crazy. "What thing, she asks. Let's see. The thing where you hold hands. Where you smile at each other like no one is watching. Where you talk with each other and for each other."

"I don't know what you're talking about." Frankie's jaw

was set and her crossed arms tightened, pushing up her boobs. I redirected my eyes.

"Oh my God, you've had sex!" Amanda declared.

Frankie threw her hands up in the air and walked away. "I'm not talking about this."

"You have."

Amanda and Juan started talking to each other as I followed Frankie. I swear nothing about our relationship was sacred, and if we were in Oleander, it would be worse. It would be on every news channel and our photos would be sprayed across every newspaper. I needed to keep Frankie away from that toxicity. Oleander was not a place for her. This was just another thing that confirmed it.

Amanda ran ahead of me and looped an arm through Frankie's.

CHAPTER FORTY

Frankie

I DIDN'T LOOK at Amanda. "This is not something I want to talk about."

"I'm sorry. I didn't mean to embarrass you." She gave my arm a squeeze. I turned to see if Sebastian and Juan were following. They were headed to the car, probably to unload. Sebastian preferred to get things done straightaway.

"How are the new horses? Did you and Juan settle them in OK?" I asked.

"Good. They're all off the track thoroughbreds. Some have been spelling longer than others."

"So, we should be able to start working with them when we get back."

I led her to her room and sat on her bed. This had been Dad's room when he was younger. Grandma had made a quilt from all of his horse ribbons. It was folded and hanging over the chair at the sturdy wooden desk. Mum would have put it there to keep it safe.

"Are you coming back?" she asked.

My head sprung up. "Why wouldn't I be coming back? I've still got one season left."

"But you don't have to. That was just something you set for yourself."

I shook my head. "There's no need to change it."

"Are you sure? I see plenty of reasons. Your dad is better now. He can start working again and you don't have to send money home. You have horses here to work with. This is where you want to be."

I hadn't thought about it until that moment. I always thought I'd go back for that last season. "Well, yeah–"

"And I'm pretty sure Sebastian would be happy to stay here with you."

"He's not going to stay here."

"Why not?"

"Because he's a crown prince. He's got better things to do with his life."

"Frankie, you are so dense sometimes. That man has been in love with you for months."

"In love with the idea of me, maybe." What had Billy said? Deflection is a form of denial. I knew what I'd just said wasn't true. I pushed myself further onto her bed and lay staring at the ceiling. Amanda lay beside me.

Only hours ago, Sebastian told me he loved me. Me. His kiss had come too quickly after that for me to digest his words. My body had had no trouble responding though. When he kissed me, my heart joined my stomach in its lurch.

"What do you mean?"

"I don't know. It doesn't matter. He'll go back to Oleander and I'll stay here."

"You could go with him."

I took a deep breath and blew it out, puffing up my cheeks. "My home is here."

WE SAT around the dinner table; Juan was promising to give Mum a tango lesson. Sebastian leaned over and whispered in my ear, "Do you think he actually knows how to do the tango?"

"Surely you've seen him do it."

"Nope. Four years and I haven't seen it once."

"Well, he'd better or else he'll have one disappointed McKenzie on his hands."

"Imagine being cut off from her brownies."

We laughed to ourselves. Amanda glanced at us. She had that all-knowing smile on her lips when she spoke up: "So, Jim, what's with the new horses? Is this your subtle way of stealing Frankie off me?"

Dad shrugged. "The opportunity arose and I thought it was the right time."

"The right time?"

"Well, yeah. She and Sebastian were coming home. They've had time to spend with the horses."

"And then they wouldn't want to leave them."

"Their thought processes are not in my control."

"Uh-huh."

Mum turned towards us. "Does that mean you're staying?"

"I hadn't really thought about it," I said.

"We would love for you to stay."

"Do you need to do another polo season?" Sebastian asked.

"It would give me a chance to save more money. Have some time to set things up. I'd have time to speak to the racing stables about retraining their horses. Drum up some interest with the polo stables."

"Like setting the foundations?"

"Yes."

I got up to clear the table. When Sebastian got up to help, I pushed him back down. I wanted to be alone. To think.

Everything was all mucked up. I had this plan for my life. I knew exactly where I would be and when. My blinkers were on and I was heading straight for the finish line. The race had been going exactly to plan. But as I turned the last corner, when that finish line was in sight, the line had moved.

Mum walked in and picked up the tea towel as I started to wash the dishes.

"Leave it. I'll do it," I said.

Mum nodded. She walked to the dining table and said, "Let's all go outside. I'll make us some coffee soon."

The chairs scraped on the floor when they got up to leave. I closed my eyes, bracing myself against the counter. How had things got so messed up? Sebastian. It was all Sebastian.

I emptied my mind as I washed the dishes. I concentrated on that task alone. Glasses. Cutlery. Plates. One by one. Washing and the drying. I cleaned the counter, wiped down the table and put the left overs away. There was nothing left to do.

I didn't have the energy to go and sit with them. I needed to think. Or not think. I wanted to ride. But they'd be able to see me from where they were sitting. I went to my room instead. Mum would come in to make coffee, find me gone and say I'd gone to bed.

After getting changed into my PJ's, I climbed under the covers and curled up. I didn't really need to do another season at the polo stables. I had enough money saved. Mum and Dad didn't need me to send money back any more. The horses needed me here. They could wait until the end of the season, live the good life until then. But I was eager to continue their training; every day they became more responsive.

This was my dream. To be home with my family. To work with horses. To be on the land I loved.

And then there was Sebastian. I loved him too. But that was just foolish. He was never going to stay. He might want to, but duty would always call him home. What I hated most about that was his impending unhappiness. I didn't want to think of him in a world bereft of love, especially when he had so much to give.

Sebastian's door opened. Boots thumped off. He placed his phone on the bedside table to charge with a click into the charger. I couldn't see him from my room but I knew exactly what he was doing. His clothes came off with a whisper through the walls. I imagined him covering his fine torso in his sleep shirt. Footsteps came into my room. The covers shifted aside as he settled in beside me and put his arm around me. I relaxed into him, enjoying the strength of his arm around me and his warmth at my back.

"Are you OK?"

I shrugged. How could I put all of my thoughts into words?

"Just because they want you to come home now it doesn't mean you have to."

"That's not the way it works for you though, is it? Even though you don't want to go home, there's no real way to avoid it."

"No, there's not."

"I hate to think of you there. Alone. No horses. No joy."

"No you."

I swallowed the lump in my throat. "When do you have to go?"

"I should have been there already. My mother expected my return after this polo season."

I felt like the air had been sucked from my lungs. Like when you fall off a horse and you hit the ground so hard all the air is expelled.

"Why haven't you asked me to go with you?"

"I don't want you there."

I stiffened. Why? Because I wasn't good enough?

"Frankie, if I could spend the rest of my life with you, I would. But I can't take you there. I can't watch the life drain out of you because you are trapped in a world with no freedom. My love for you would never compensate for what you'd have to give up, what you'd have to endure."

He was willing to suffer alone to save me.

Tears stung my eyes. I rolled over and cupped his face.

"I love you, Sebastian."

He closed his eyes as if he were savouring the words. When he kissed me, I felt the power of his love in that kiss. My heart and every cell in my body felt like it had found its equilibrium.

CHAPTER FORTY-ONE

Sebastian

"Why don't we go for a ride today?" I suggested at breakfast.

"Yes, we can get a look at this bush Frankie is always talking about," Juan said.

Frankie smiled. "We can visit the big dam and have a swim."

We finished breakfast and tacked up the horses. It had only been a few days since the rain but already new growth was evident. Small tufts of grass were sprouting between rocks and along the soft edges of the track. The leaves on the trees were more vibrant, like the dust had been washed away.

Life surrounded us. Birds were singing a concerto. Small birds, bell birds and the willy wagtails Frankie had told me about, tweeted a constant undercurrent. Crows, with their deep caws, sounded every now and then, adding emphasis.

"Listen," Frankie said. "Can you hear that bird? It's singing 'did you get drunk?'"

We rode in silence, listening hard. The bird sang. *Did you get drunk? Did you get drunk?* We laughed. And listened. And laughed some more, like children.

We approached some small trees about two metres in height. Their branches were like lightning strikes pointing in all directions. I examined the leaves as we got closer; they were like tiny spikes. Not like the flat oblong leaves of the gum trees around them. Frankie cut off a stem and twirled it in her hand before passing it to me. "Have a smell of it."

It was like a mixture of pine and eucalyptus. I breathed the refreshing scent in deeper before passing it to Juan.

"It's melaleuca, more commonly known as tea tree," Frankie explained. "Aboriginals have used it for thousands of years. When they had a toothache, they'd chew the leaves into a pulp and rest it on their tooth and gums."

Juan passed it to Amanda, who took a deep breath in.

"They used it for coughs and colds and treated wounds with it, especially bites and stings."

"Didn't the soldiers in World War Two have it in their first aid kits?" Amanda asked.

"Yeah, it was great for insect bites and as an antifungal."

I tore off a small branch and stuck it in my saddle bag. Something to remember the Australian bush by.

Even though Frankie and I vowed to enjoy every moment together, the fact that I would have to leave hung over my head. And I knew I had to do it soon. Not just because my mother continued to pester me. I needed to go and face it. On my terms.

We continued our ride with Frankie in the lead. I was hoping to see another goanna to show Juan but none were to be seen. There was lots of scurrying in the leaf litter which I thought must have been lizards. We'd often see them at the farm sunning themselves.

When we entered a paddock, Frankie pointed to a dam. "How about a race?"

There was no way I was passing up an opportunity for a gallop. "What's in it for the winner?"

"Depends on who the winner is."

She took off, her brown pony tail flying behind her. I kicked my horse into action. She was more than willing to go. I was flung back. Pressing my feet down into the stirrups I forced my body forward. Amanda and Juan were right beside me. We were gaining on Frankie. At least, I thought we were, but she and Jane moved like the wind, as if with no effort at all. Frankie didn't even look back. She had the target in her sights and she aimed straight for it. When she got to the dam wall, she jumped off Jane in one fluid motion and turned to us. Her smiled beamed, like sunlight breaking through clouds. I would never get enough of that smile.

"What kept you?" she said when we arrived.

I followed her to the water's edge where she stripped down to her bikini. I sighed imagining what I would do to her if we didn't have company.

I peered at the water. "It's brown."

"Yeah. It's a dam."

"Is there anything living in there?"

"Not likely."

"Do you swim here a lot?"

"Nearly all summer long as kids."

She walked in. Goosebumps erupted on her skin. Juan and Amanda headed up the other end and stripped off, distracted with their chatter. I shrugged. No point putting it off. I stripped down to my boxers and followed Frankie. As soon as I was in up to chest height, she waded over to me. My hands found her hips and drifted up to her breasts. The water on her skin glistened. She wrapped her legs around my waist. I grabbed her butt and pulled her closer so she settled down on my hardness.

Her gasp made me smile.

She reached her hand to my face and moved my shaggy hair from my eyes. "I love your hair. Some days it's like an unruly child."

She bent her face closer to mine. Her teeth teased my lips before she kissed me. She sank lower. The only things separating us were two thin pieces of material and my dick didn't really care. I imagined us being skin to skin.

"Frankie," I moaned into her mouth as she pushed against me.

She pulled away from me, her eyes half closed, her lips red from our heated kissing. She smiled. "Yes, Sebastian?"

"We need to stop." Amanda and Juan were only metres away.

"Really?" She pulled herself closer. I wanted to rip that material aside and plunge into her right there. "Only if you promise to make up for it later."

"Without a doubt."

"Well, alright then." She unwrapped her legs and gave me a light kiss. Floating on her back, her breasts fell slightly to the side and her body glistened in brown dam water, ready for the taking. I would take her alright, just not here.

CHAPTER FORTY-TWO

Frankie

We passed Mum and Dad on the way back. They were heading out in the ute to check the cows and calves. After untacking the horses, we gave them a feed and headed into the house.

"We should shower," I said to Sebastian. "You can use the downstairs bathroom," I said to Amanda and Juan. They gave each other a knowing smile.

"Sure," Juan said, giving Amanda a wink.

"Oh yeah, we wouldn't want to disturb you."

"And we don't want to hear you."

"We don't need the sort of education you gave that calf." Amanda laughed at her own joke.

I shook my head and made my way upstairs.

Sebastian followed me into the bathroom, locking the door behind him. "Time to make it up to you."

My heart galloped as he approached me from behind. His hand wrapped around my hip, firm and strong, anchoring me to the spot. His other hand swept my hair off my neck. Warm lips kissed my neck sending tingles down my spine.

Sebastian's hand drifted around the front and pulled me closer to him. His hardness pressed into me and my desire left my lips as they whispered his name. His other hand found my breast and massaged it through the layers of my clothing. I arched my back, pushing myself against his dick. His composure cracked for a brief moment when he sucked in a breath.

His hands moved away from my body and tugged at my t-shirt, pulling it over my head. The clasp of my bikini top released and he slipped the straps off my shoulder, letting it fall to the ground. I turned to face him but he forced me back into place.

One hand cupped my breast as the other undid the button of my jeans and slid the zip down. His hand found its way into my underwear and the wetness between my folds. I ground myself against his hand as he teased my nipples with his other hand. Desire blossomed as he kissed me behind the ear.

I needed him inside me. His fingers. His dick. Anything. I yanked at my jeans.

"Let me." He spun me around and claimed my lips before his hands took hold of my hips. The way he held me made me feel like I was his and his alone. His lips moved to my breasts and he sucked on one nipple and then the other. They made their way lower. Each kiss along my stomach sent a tremble through my body. Sebastian pulled my jeans down and helped me step out of them before his lips reached my inner thigh.

"You smell so good. Like Frankie mixed with dam water."

My breath hitched as his tongue made its way up my leg.

His hand nudged my legs open. A finger circled my opening before delving into the wetness and circling the inside.

It wasn't enough. I needed him.

"Sebastian." His name ended in a moan as a second finger entered me.

"Mmmm." His tongue tasted me.

"I need you inside me."

His fingers moved. "I am inside you."

I closed my legs on his hand. His fingers slipped out and played in between my folds instead.

"I'm only trying to make it up to you," he mumbled between licks.

"Sebastian."

His fingers teased as his mouth made its way back to mine.

"What do you want Frankie?" He whispered in my ear.

"You."

CHAPTER FORTY-THREE

Sebastian

I LIFTED Frankie up and she wrapped her legs around me. I'd never wanted someone so much in my life. In every way possible. Our lips met, both as hungry as the other. Not breaking our kiss, I carried her to the bathroom bench and set her down. Frankie reached for my shirt and lifted it over my head before undoing my jeans. I shoved them down and as I stood up straight, I entered her in one fluid motion.

Her body swayed as I moved in and out. Our chests met and retreated in perfect rhythm. The softness of her breasts caressed me. I watched, mesmerised, as they spread wide each time they were compressed.

Our lips fell apart and hers parted with heavy breaths. I wanted them back, on mine, to taste them for the rest of my days.

My hand entangled itself in her thick hair, dried and clumped from swimming in the dam. Frankie rested her head in my hand, exposing her neck. I sucked on it, enjoying the earthiness left from the dam water. Her breasts pushed against me as she let out a moan. I drove into her harder, my legs banging against the cabinet doors. Her fingers dug into my shoulders. I held her closer, making sure my full length was inside her, pumping. I could feel sweat drip down my spine.

Frankie's lips searched for mine, uncontrolled, like our momentum as I emptied myself inside her. Her sigh followed her moan. My legs shook and I rested them against the cabinet doors to steady myself.

We held each other close, kissing, until our raw desire melted away. When I regained my strength, I pulled away and helped Frankie off the bench. She ran her hands down my body until she reached my jeans that had slipped down to my knees and helped me out of them. Her lips returned to mine and she brushed them lightly before leading me to the shower. "We came here to shower, remember."

"If we did that every time we showered, I'd shower five times a day."

She smiled at me as she turned the water on. The hot water hit my shoulders and ran down my body. Frankie's soaped up hands did the same. This was intimacy at the next level. She washed every inch of my skin, stopping at each muscle to explore it. I memorised everything. Her touch. Her look of admiration. The feel of her tongue as she licked water off my body. The way she smiled at me. Her wet lashes framed her hazel eyes as she looked up at me. I memorized the whiteness of her belly that rarely saw the sun and the way it contrasted with her tanned arms. I needed to remember it all so it could accompany me when I was alone at night.

CHAPTER FORTY-FOUR

Frankie

"AMANDA, can you and Juan do follow the leader with us please?" Livvy asked. We sat on the sun bed with the twins while Noah and Sarah played in the sandpit. Sebastian was talking with Juan near the horses.

Amanda eyeballed me, her hand open and her head tilted in a 'what is she talking about' gesture.

"Sebastian made up an obstacle course and we all have to follow his instructions."

Amanda turned her attention to the twins. "Sounds like fun. Go and get Uncle Sebastian."

They ran off, holding hands giggling, and collected the younger kids on the way. Amanda turned to me. "I don't know who is going to miss Uncle Sebastian more, you or them."

"Me." I hated to think about it. Every day we had together was a blessing. But every day brought us closer to the day he'd have to leave. I watched the children as they approached Sebastian and his wide smile in response to what they said.

"Uh-huh. So, you do love him."

"Only a stupid person would fall in love with a crown prince who was destined to leave."

"I would never say you're stupid, Frankie."

"Well, my heart is."

Sebastian and Juan made their way to the shed with the four kids in tow.

"He'd make a great dad."

"I hope he gets to experience that one day. He deserves happiness." Tears stung my eyes and an ice pick stabbed my heart. It ached like the punctures were disabling one chamber at a time.

"You deserve happiness too."

"I will be happy. I'll be where I always wanted to be. Doing what I always wanted."

"Alone."

"Like I always wanted."

The kids approached us. The young ones carried one of Dad's fishing nets between them. What on earth did Sebastian have planned? I smiled at Sarah and Noah as they struggled with their haul. Both wore huge grins.

"We going to have so much fun," Noah said. They stopped in front of us but kept hold of their precious cargo.

"I bet we are," I said.

Tilly carried a tarp and Livvy sat in a wheelbarrow that Juan was pushing. He gave me a shrug when Sebastian arrived with a jumble of shovels, rakes and brooms. He laid the obstacle course out and pegged the net down to the ground.

We made our way through the course as knights on horseback, ninjas practicing our balancing skills on the handles of the equipment, spies disguising ourselves as logs rolling along the grass and stopping on demand, strongmen pushing four kids at once in the wheelbarrow, long distance swimmers crossing the English Channel (aka the tarp). There were excited squeals and peals of laughter. And then we arrived at the net.

Sebastian stood beside it and regarded each child in turn. "This obstacle is one requiring great skill. Many have tried to pass but failed. Each young soldier in training needs to crawl under this net until they find freedom on the other side."

The children held hands and eyed the net laid out before them. They looked at Sebastian for further instructions.

"Now remember, this isn't a race. It's about teamwork."

The older girls raised their hands in the air as a show of power. The young ones did the same. I laughed. They all had such determined looks on their faces, their characters shining through.

"To the net," Sebastian shouted. "On your knees. On your bellies. Go."

The twins held up the net so the younger pair could shimmy under. Once their bodies were in position, they joined them. It wasn't easy going because hands and feet got tangled in the net. Progress was slow but they were advancing. We all stood by, encouraging them.

Sebastian's phone rang. He pulled it out of his pocket, stuck it on silent and put it back in. Noah got stuck. His hand came through the net and somehow got twisted. Sarah was trapped beside him. Sebastian's watch screen started flashing. He pressed the ignore button. Noah started crying. Sarah echoed him. Sebastian's phone started again.

"Bastan, help," Noah called out.

"I'm stuck. Help," Sarah cried.

"Stuck here forever," Noah declared, with only the drama a four-year-old could muster.

Sarah wailed.

Sebastian's phone rang again.

"Shit." He took the phone out and shoved it in our direction. I think he was aiming for Juan, but it landed in my hands instead. "Can you answer it please?"

The crying continued. I pressed answer and walked away from the noise. "Hello, Sebastian's phone, Frankie speaking."

Silence on the phone. Dramatic pleas from behind me.

"We've failed. We won't pass our soldier test."

"I'm sorry, who's speaking?" an uptight voice said on the other end of the line.

"This is Frankie."

"Don't be ridiculous, Uncle Sebastian won't let us fail."

I took a quick glance over my shoulder. Sebastian was subduing the children, chortling at their antics.

"This is Queen Meredith of Oleander. I'd like to speak to my son, Crown Prince Sebastian."

I was taken aback by her curtness.

Cheering erupted.

"Uncle Sebastian saved us. He deserves a medal."

I walked further away from the excited cries and wails. Sebastian was comforting Sarah, a bemused smile on his face.

"I'm sorry. He can't come to the phone at the moment. Can I take a message for him?"

"I would like to speak to my son, Crown Prince Sebastian."

Dread as heavy as lead settled over me at her cold voice.

"I understand that, but he can't speak right now. I'm sorry."

"I suggest you inform him that the Queen is requesting to speak to him about his imminent return home."

She wasn't taking no for an answer. But I couldn't very well interrupt him when he was trying to calm Sarah down. Things could go from bad to worse.

"Now would be the appropriate time to do that," she added.

Wow, talk about entitled. I was not one of her servants who would bow down to her wishes. "You'll need to wait until he is available."

Sarah soothed. Sebastian handed her over to Juan who held her tight.

"Where are you going, Uncle Sebastian?" Tilly called out.

Silence on the phone.

"I just need to take this call and I'll be right back."

I handed the phone to him. I would have preferred to smash it on the ground. "It's the queen."

CHAPTER FORTY-FIVE

Sebastian

THE HAPPINESS that had filled me disappeared. I took Frankie's hand and gave it a squeeze. More to strengthen me than anything else. Breathing in deep I tried to calm my nerves.

"Hello, Mother."

"Sebastian, where are you? Who is Frankie?"

"I'm in Australia." *Just like I was last month and the month before that,* I added to myself.

"Still in Australia. The polo season has ended." The frustration in her voice was clear.

I turned towards the giggling children. Amanda and Juan were distracting them by making funny faces.

"What was all that noise in the background? Why are those children calling you Uncle Sebastian?"

"We were playing a game. It went awry." Why was I telling her this? She didn't care. She was only digging for information.

"Your brother is engaged."

Well, at least one of us might find happiness.

"To Lady Lucinda of Reachert."

Or not.

"The engagement celebration is in ten days. I expect you to be here."

Ten days. My dream life only had a few days left to run.

"OK."

"It's high time you resumed your royal duties."

"Yes, Mother."

She disconnected.

I took Frankie in my arms and held her tight.

"When?"

"A few days." She stiffened. I'd stall as long as I could but I needed to get back in time to be fitted for a new suit and be prepped for my duties on the day.

She pulled away from my embrace. She didn't look at me as she said, "Let's finish the game."

I watched her walk away realising I'd soon be walking away, too—from all of this. This would be one of the last days I spent with her, with them, here. Picking my heart up off the floor, I followed her.

CHAPTER FORTY-SIX

Frankie

WE ALL SAT around the dinner table. Sarah insisted on sitting on her hero's lap, and Sebastian took it in stride like he always did. I knew he was preparing to tell them all he was leaving. He'd hardly touched his food and didn't join in the conversation. In a way, I wished he wouldn't. It was like as soon as the words were out there, it would be final.

When there was a lull in the conversation he said, "I'll be leaving in two days. I'm going back to Oleander."

The lull transformed into a deathly silence. Everyone turned to Sebastian. Livvy went to say something but Louise put a firm hand on her shoulder. Mum and Dad looked at each other in that way married couples do, having a silent conversation. Juan and Amanda stared at their plates. I grabbed Sebastian's hand under the table.

"Two days?" Mum asked, her voice shaky. Dad rested his hand on hers on top of the table.

"Yes, my mother called to tell me of my brother's engagement. I need to return for the celebration."

"And then you're coming back?" Billy asked. He'd set his knife and fork down.

"I don't know...I don't think so."

I knew he'd paused because he didn't want to make promises he couldn't keep. I clenched my teeth. I tried to breathe in deep to calm my racing heart but it was too difficult with my jaw taut. Breathing won.

I glanced at the twins sitting next to Louise. They'd followed the conversation closely and were looking at their mum with tears brimming in their eyes. She was talking to them quietly. They kept shaking their heads.

"Are you going with him?" Dad asked me.

I sat up tall in my chair. I was confident in my answer. The only thing I'd been confident in since the phone call yesterday. "No. This is my home."

"Two days," Brady mumbled. "It's so soon. Billy and I had so much planned for you."

I bit the inside of my cheek. The pain distracted me from crying. There was no point. We were fooling ourselves if we thought this was never going to happen. Sebastian had always been honest with us. But it hadn't stopped my whole family from falling in love with him.

Louise took the two girls to the loungeroom to talk to them. Words drifted to us as she told them Sebastian still loved them and they could still be a part of his life. Their protests died, replaced with quiet whispers devising a strategy to keep in touch. The twins were six and I'm sure their hearts would mend much faster than mine.

We all resumed eating. I found it hard to swallow my

food. I shifted it around my plate instead. The normal conversation had died away and it was unlike any family meal I'd ever had. Even when Granma had died, we reminisced over the good times we'd had with her. We had laughed then, despite our hearts being filled with sadness.

CHAPTER FORTY-SEVEN

Sebastian

Frankie and I stood outside the paddock and watched the horses. The mare and foal had returned to the herd the day before. There had been no problems. Frankie had been confident there wouldn't be. All the horses had whinnied and nickered to each other over the fence in the two weeks we'd been home.

When they went into the paddock, the other horses approached the mare and foal straight away, sniffing and nuzzling. The foal introduced itself to the other horses. When it had enough of the curious nudging, it ran away, bucking and jumping. The mare stood with her herd, grazing.

"Are you ready?" Frankie asked.

I nodded. Every part of the property I said goodbye to, I left a little bit of my heart behind. We walked around to the front of the house where everyone was waiting. Frankie walked past them and waited for me beside the car. Amanda went and stood beside her and took her hand.

I swallowed the lump in my throat as I turned to the twins. Tears streamed down their faces. I crouched and took them into my arms.

"I love you, Uncle Sebastian."

My throat hurt as I tried to hold back my tears. "I love you too, Livvy. And you, Tilly."

"Mum said we could Facetime you."

"Every day if you want."

"You won't be too busy for us now that you're going to be a prince again?"

"Never. If I miss your call, I'll always call you back."

"Promise?"

"Promise."

That was one promise I could keep. I stood up. Louise hugged me tight, crushing Noah between us. He let go of her and flung his arms around my neck. Sarah, not wanting to miss out, launched herself out of Billy's arms. I laughed as I hugged them tight. Billy patted me on the back before retrieving his child.

"Well, there goes any chance of marrying Frankie off."

Brady chimed in. "Yeah, no one in this country is crazy enough to have her."

They both embraced me. I didn't want Frankie to marry anyone else. But what did I expect her to do, wait for someone who would likely never return?

I walked to Margaret and Jim, the parents I wished I had. Jim removed his arm from her shoulder as Margaret took a step towards me. She cupped my face in that special way she had with her soft but strong hands. "I'll pray every day for your safe return."

Tears ignored my attempts to hold them in and rolled

down my cheeks. She was what a mother should be – loving, caring, understanding. And here she was hoping I'd return into her fold. I could only dream her prayers would make a difference. That I would come back here, where my heart belonged. But it was impossible. My mother would never let me leave again.

Jim approached.

"Even though you're leaving, we are proud to consider you a part of our family," he said gruffly as he pulled me into a quick embrace.

I stood tall as he released me and smiled. "That's a bit different to your threats of maiming me."

He laughed and patted my shoulder. I turned and took one last look at them before walking to the car.

CHAPTER FORTY-EIGHT

Frankie

I stood in the bathroom of our motel room, bracing myself. Sebastian was waiting for me. Soon he'd be leaving for a home and life he didn't want. For a home and life I didn't want him to have.

But this wasn't about me. All of his life no one had been there to support him. I wanted him to know that no matter what decision he made I would still love him.

His bodyguards would be here in minutes. I pushed myself away from the sink and strode out to where he sat on the bed. His cases, which we had packed the day before, were beside the door, waiting.

"Ready?" I asked.

"No."

"Me either." I sat down beside him. "Sebastian, I'm sorry all of your choices have been taken away from you." I took a deep breath. That's not what I'd wanted to say.

He took hold of my hand, giving me the courage to look at him.

"If you get back home and you decide that's the right place for you to be, I want you to know I support that decision. I support you."

He reached out to trace my lips with his fingertips and then leant over to kiss me. I kissed him back, leaving all the promises unmade, the impossible future, my ever-burning love in that one kiss. This man, who was so much more than a prince, showed me a love I never knew existed.

"Juan warned me not to fall for you. Not to pursue you. But his warning came months too late. I was gone the day you scowled at the NDA," Sebastian said.

I smiled. I should frame that damn NDA. It led me to him but the premise behind it tore him away.

"Does Juan still think that you should have stayed away?"

"No." He smiled and tears swelled in his eyes. "Now he thinks I waited too long."

A knock interrupted us. Sebastian's bodyguards opened the door and took his cases. I stood with Sebastian and held him one last time. I tried to memorise everything in that last moment. His strong arms, his earthy scent, the way he whispered "I love you" before he let me go and walked out the door.

I took the letter out that he had given me the night before and read it for the first time.

ONCE UPON A TIME there was a prince. He visited a place called Australia. Beauty was everywhere, nature abounded and bird songs welcomed every day. It was a treasured place with a short but interesting history. He loved it and the people so much he never wanted to leave.

The prince met a fair lady there. Her name was Frankie. She was as beautiful as beautiful can be. When she laughed the entire world lit up. Prince Sebastian fell in love with her. But the fair lady denied him for many months.

Prince Sebastian visited her home. That's when he fell in love with her family as well. They were just like Frankie – full of life and love. They teased each other and made jokes. They ate together and talked about their day. Each and every one of them cared for the others. Laughter filled their home and it was unlike anything he had ever experienced.

With all of his being he wanted to stay with that family. He had never felt so much love as he had in those days he spent there. And the fair lady gave him understanding and a strength he never expected.

Happily ever after seemed impossible. But he would do everything he could to find a way. And it seemed possible now because Frankie showed him who he could become.

I crawled into the bed and hugged his pillow to me. The quiet tears turned into sobs that wracked my body.

"HOW DID IT GO?" Amanda asked when I walked into the house we shared at the polo stables.

"Fine."

She peered at me like she wanted more.

"What do you want me to say? We both broke down crying? Well, we didn't. We knew this day would come."

"Yes. Sebastian had no choice. He had to return," Juan said. "But I don't blame him for staying away for so long."

"What do you mean?" Amanda asked.

"I went there once with him. I didn't like it."

"You went to the castle?"

Listening, I sat on the arm of the couch. Sebastian hadn't told me much about his home.

"*Si*. We went to visit for a week, in the castle."

"What was it like?"

"It was beautiful. What you would see in a magazine. But cold and lifeless."

Just as Sebastian had described it.

"Who was there?"

"The queen and king."

I sat still, taking it all in. I let Amanda ask the questions for me. I didn't trust my voice.

"Were they nice?"

"They tried their best to be polite. But I did not feel comfortable."

I wanted to get up and leave. I didn't want to hear anymore.

"His bodyguards were always around. Not upstairs in the castle, of course. But downstairs where the workers were. We spent a lot of time down there. Sebastian said it had always been his secret hideaway."

There, it wasn't all bad. He did have a place to escape to.

"I'm going to pack," I said, getting up and heading to my room. I sat on my bed and stared at the walls that had been mine for the past five years. They were plain white once but I'd added team photos and ribbons from some of our winning matches, dotting the wall with colour. It was bittersweet to be leaving. This had become my second home and Amanda was like a sister. The thought I wouldn't see her every day was strange. We lived together and worked together but did not tire of each other. Of course, we had moments where we couldn't stand the sight of the other but that never lasted long. Only because she was less stubborn than me.

I undid all the bedding and bundled it up into a big pile on the bed. Then started on the chest of drawers. Amanda came in to help and started on the wardrobe. "It's going to be weird without you here."

"I know. Is Juan going to stay long?"

"He said he can stay a few weeks and help with the horses. That will give me time to find someone new."

"That's good."

"I think it will keep his mind off Sebastian. It's going to be hard for him."

"Yeah. They've been together for four years."

"They're probably closer than us."

What was I going to do to keep my mind off Sebastian? Work, I guess. I had plenty to do to set up the property for my horse retraining. Most of the infrastructure was there, but I needed to fence some more paddocks off and electrify some for stallions and colts waiting to be gelded or difficult horses. The round yard needed some touch ups and more rubber. I needed to make cavalettis and jumps for the training phase. And I wanted to put in a sand arena.

"Will you be OK?" she asked, breaking through my distraction.

"Why wouldn't I be? I've got everything I want."

"Except Sebastian."

"That was never going to last. He had to go home at some point."

I walked out of the room with a box, ending the conversation.

CHAPTER FORTY-NINE

Sebastian

We drove through the capital's streets heading for the castle. Frankie would love these old buildings. When we had been in Maryborough, I had marvelled at the structures, eclectic in their architecture.

None of those buildings compared in age to the ones we were passing. The ones in my home city had all been built and designed in the same era, meaning they had conformity. They were tall with spires or fancy gables, all some type of muted brown or yellow. The ones in Maryborough ranged in period and design. They were impressive but on a different level. Where the city of Maryborough had seen a demise of sorts and was rebuilding itself to its former glory, the capital of Oleander had never known such hardship. Its streets were always perfectly kept and its buildings the epitome of wealth.

What was Frankie doing? The day had just started in Australia. I imagined the first morning rays filtering through the curtains and Frankie ignoring them as she always did, trying to catch some more sleep. I'd texted her to say I'd arrived but had received no answer.

"It must be good to be back, Prince Sebastian," our driver said.

"Yes." I was playing my part. My true thoughts and feelings must be kept within. My mask was to stay firmly in place. It already felt exhausting.

We drove through the castle gates. I examined the castle from my seat in the back. The three-story, hard-angled structure was cold and imposing. Just as the hearts inside were.

The Rolls Royce stopped at the enormous front doors. I reached out to grab the handle but my bodyguard stopped me. I needed to remember my place in the world. One of my status wouldn't open their own door. I gave him a grateful smile. Once I stepped inside, my companions would leave me.

My mother and father did not greet me at the door or the entrance hall. Of course, they wouldn't. This was not like Frankie's family who welcomed you with open arms or some smart comment.

I walked into the rich wooden entrance hall that towered above me. The cold marble floor led to a grand staircase directly facing the entrance. Its banisters were gilded; there would be no sliding down those. At the top of the staircase was a bust of the queen warmly lit. It was the only warm thing about her.

I found them in the sitting room. Plush sofas surrounded the fire place. Round side tables held ancient ceramic vases and statues. Mother approached me dressed in her pale pink two-piece suit. Who wears a suit in their own home to welcome their son on his return? The Queen, of course. Her light brown hair was impeccable, tied back at the nape of her neck, not a hair out of place. She accepted a kiss on each cheek. My lips did not connect. It was all for show. She studied me; her mouth turned down. "Your hair is unacceptable. I will arrange the barber."

"No need. My hair will stay as it is."

She pursed her lips, but said nothing more. Edward approached. At least he was dressed more casually in designer jeans and t-shirt. Smiling, he held out his hand. "Welcome home, Sebastian."

"Thank you, Edward. Congratulations on your engagement."

"Thank you. Lucinda is looking forward to seeing you again."

I wasn't so sure I was looking forward to seeing her. The last time we'd met, we were forced to dance together at a ball. She was unimpressed with my form. But I guess she was not to blame for her behaviour. While she was firmly instructed and adhered to societal rules, I had no interest in them.

"Will she be coming to dinner tonight?" I asked.

"Actually, no. Mother needed to ensure you had not regressed into a heathen before she introduced you to anyone outside the family." Edward smiled at me. Was my brother trying to be funny? I had never witnessed such a thing.

Mother turned on her heel and walked off. Father, his hair now more grey than brown, patted my shoulder on the way past.

"You should probably freshen up before dinner," Edward said. "Try to give some indication that you've contemplated life."

He followed them out of the room. I didn't understand what was happening. Or maybe I did. My younger brother had always helped me in social situations. Was this his way of showing me he still had my back? I shook my head.

My suite hadn't changed. Gold mirrors hung on the rich burgundy walls, surrounding beautifully crafted furniture and plush bedding. An enormous thick rug gave warmth to the wooden floor. I tried to picture Frankie here with me, sitting on the bed, examining the room. I pushed the image away. She didn't belong here.

But I did belong with her. That much I knew.

I showered before making my way to the dining room. I sat in silence while my mother spoke of the engagement celebration. As much as it was about Edward and Lucinda, it was also about my introduction back into society. What I really wanted to talk about was Edward and his betrothed, but every time I tried to shift the conversation, I was shut down.

When my parents left, I closed my eyes and gave a silent thank you to whoever was looking down on me.

"You seem different," Edward said.

"So do you."

"You don't want to be here, do you?"

"No." There was no point lying.

"Why did you come back?"

I looked at him across the table. His expression was open and curious, eyebrows lifted up, inviting me to speak.

"I could have stayed away but returning to Oleander would always hang over my head. How could I build a future for myself knowing I would have to return someday?"

"So, you feel you didn't have a choice?"

"No choice. Only duty."

CHAPTER FIFTY

Frankie

I WAITED for the house to quiet before I slipped out of bed for a shower and breakfast. I didn't want to endure the looks of sympathy or the questions about Sebastian. I hadn't called him even though he'd been gone for days. It was too hard.

I walked out to the horse paddock, where the horses were happily eating their hay. Dad must have fed them. I could hear Mum and the two youngest children in the house yard behind me. Opening the gate, I went to say hello to the horses. I'd let them eat and rest before I worked with them. But I needed my morning horse fix.

The gelding trotted up to me. He'd been more affectionate with me since Sebastian had left. He came right up into my personal space, his legs beside mine, and lowered his head. Giving him long pats, I rested my head against him. I breathed him in, lost in that moment, feeling at peace. I didn't want to move and the gelding stood with me.

"Go eat. I'll be back soon," I said, giving him a last pat.

I walked to the stable where I'd stacked some copper logs I was going to paint for trot and jump poles. Lining two up about one and a half metres apart, I then rolled four on top. I did the same with another pair so I could paint eight at a time. Then I went to the storeroom and pulled out a can of paint. The painting was time-consuming but the rhythmic strokes helped calm my mind. Thoughts of Sebastian creeped in and I imagined him painting with me, coordinating his brush strokes with mine. I pushed the image out of my mind. He wasn't here. He wasn't going to come back. And I'd never see him again. There was nothing I could do about it.

I stood up and stretched. My legs were aching from crouching for so long. My mouth was dry. Stupid me had forgotten to bring a drink bottle. Walking back to the house, I passed the children in the sandpit. Thankfully, they didn't notice me. They'd been asking for days to do the obstacle course. I couldn't get it through their heads that I would never do one with them again.

When I walked back downstairs with my water bottle the children were nowhere to be seen. As I neared the stable, I could hear them. The paint was not where I'd left it. With my heart rate increasing I looked around in panic.

I'd been gone just a few minutes and they'd wreaked havoc like only a three- and four-year-old could.

There were white hand prints all over the stable door. The ground was plastered with foot prints. One look at the paint past their ankles told me they'd dipped their feet in the tin. They were so engrossed in their artistic endeavours they hadn't heard me step up behind them.

"What are you doing?"

Noah turned around, his hands dripping with paint.

White globs flicked everywhere: over my clothes, my face, my hair.

"Aunny Frannie, we painting."

"Stop that now! You can't just go around painting things."

"It's pretty," Sarah said, looking at her handiwork all google-eyed.

"Jane is pretty too," Noah said pointing.

Jane stood at the fence. Her brown belly covered in hand prints.

"You know you're not allowed to go near the horses alone." My voice was rising. "She could have kicked you. And it wouldn't have been her fault."

I grabbed them both by the wrist and yanked them away from the stable. When I turned, I saw that they had pushed my logs into the grass and dirt. I held tight against their squirming. "What is wrong with you? Can't you leave anything alone?"

"Frankie, what's going on?" Mum said as she approached us.

"Take your grandchildren and get them out of my sight. I'm sick of them. They ruin everything." I shoved them towards her.

"Frankie–"

"All I ask is that I be left alone. Is that too much to ask?"

Sarah and Noah were showing Mum their hands. They couldn't care less about the mess they'd made.

"Frankie–"

"No, Mum. I'm sick of it." My head swung from side to side like a wild woman. "How many times do they need to be told? They painted Jane. What if she got a fright and kicked one of them? What then?"

I was ranting. Why was nothing ever easy? Tears poured down my cheeks and I didn't even care.

"Just take them. Please."

Mum turned away with the children.

"Why Aunny Frannie crying?" Noah asked.

"You left a big mess for her."

"We help clean."

"That's not a good idea, sweetie. We should leave Aunty Frankie alone."

I turned my back on them and snatched up the paint brush that had been cast into the grass. So what if they thought I was weak? It was their fault I fell in love with Sebastian. If they had never invited him here, there would have been no us. I was sick of them. All of them. With their understanding glances and exaggerated gentleness, as if I was going to break. Well guess what? They just fucking broke me.

CHAPTER FIFTY-ONE

Sebastian

MOTHER WAS WAITING in the sitting room with the royal tailor. He stood up as I entered, his wiry glasses matching his frame. He approached and gave a slight nod of his head.

"Good morning Prince Sebastian." He smiled and waited as my mother approached.

Being called Prince after all these years made me feel uncomfortable. It would be another thing I needed to become accustomed to. But if I were honest, it would probably be one of the easier things. My lack of freedom was weighing on me. I hadn't left the grounds since my return, as I knew that I would be followed everywhere.

"Manuel, please fit Prince Sebastian in a tuxedo for Prince Edward's engagement. He will also require suits for when he attends parliament and other official duties."

"Yes, Your Highness."

Manuel was diligent and efficient in his duties. His assistant came in through one of the French doors with an array of fabrics. Manuel said he would make shirts for me to suit my athletic build. It was his polite way of saying my broad shoulders did not fit the family norm. Mother watched the whole time. If I wanted to make a request, she would have to approve. As it was, I couldn't be bothered. They were only clothes.

When they left, she ordered me to follow her into her office. Ordered, not asked. She indicated to the chair in front of her desk. I chose to stand. Her set jaw showed me that she disapproved. I ignored it. She took a piece of paper from a leather folder and handed it to me, then she held me in place with her steady gaze.

"The engagement will be your introduction back into society. What I have handed to you is your schedule for the week following the engagement."

I skimmed it. I would open parliament on the upcoming Monday and had meetings with the president and other high-ranking officials.

"I will appoint you a parliamentary advisor and a court liaison. I have briefed them on their duties. You are expected to become familiar with legislation. It will be your responsibility going forward to approve proposed laws."

I took a deep breath. Legislation, the running of the country, the ability to declare war on other nations, held no interest to me. But it was necessary for my role.

My role. I needed to make this work for me.

"Thank you for your forethought and preparation. In the future I would prefer to hire my own staff."

She pursed her lips. "You are not capable of making such decisions."

Her words cut like a sword. I stood resolute, unflappable.

"I would also like to spend a portion of my time as ambassador for several charities."

"As the Crown Prince, your primary role is to contribute to the running of this country."

"Yes, you have never ceased to remind me of that. However, I would like to find some balance. I believe it will assist me in becoming a better leader."

"Your humanitarian ways are not what this country needs. Nor is your type of leadership. We are not dealing with four-legged animals here with brains that can barely function. We keep a tight rein on this country for the benefit of all our people."

I recoiled at the harshness of her voice, and she persisted.

"This country has flourished under my reign. I will make you into the leader they need. Charity, animals, and *love* do not fit into that."

My heart crumpled. I had thought standing would help me invoke some sort of power. But that power was torn away with the lash of her words.

I kept my face passive. I nodded to her and, before leaving the room, I said, "Thank you, Queen."

This was my life now and I would need to fight for my soul every day.

MY PHONE RANG. My heart skipped a beat as I reached for it hoping it was Frankie. It had been five days and I'd not heard a word from her. I didn't know whether to give her space or to ring her again. Regardless, I couldn't rely on her for my happiness. I needed to learn to be as happy as I could be, even though my heart remained with Frankie. She deserved the chance to move on. No matter how unfair it was of me, I needed her, even if it was only for a little while longer.

My heart dropped when it wasn't her number on my screen.

I answered the video call putting on a big smile. "Tilly, Livvy."

"Uncle Sebastian," they called out in unison. Louise must have been holding the phone because it wasn't swinging around wildly for a change. After the first couple of phone calls where the phone kept getting snatched by the twins, she'd taken over. They still bustled to make sure they were in shot but it was much improved.

Tilly and Livvy sat on the couch side by side in short pyjamas. One in pink, the other purple.

"You wouldn't believe what happened today," Tilly said.

I sat on my bed and stared out the window at the blue sky. "What?"

"I got an award for reading."

"Did you really?"

She held the award up to the screen. "Yeah. It's because I'm getting better at it. I reckon it's because I get to read to you every night. I didn't like reading much before that."

"That's terrific. I'm so proud of you."

"Mum got to come to the assembly. Nan looked after Noah and Sarah so she could come."

I smiled to myself. I could imagine the two little rascals running amok in the school hall. Louise wouldn't have been able to enjoy herself while trying to keep them still.

"You wouldn't believe what Sarah and Noah did!" Livvy said, dramatically.

"What?"

"They made Aunty Frankie cry."

I tried to keep my voice calm. "Why did Aunty Frankie cry?"

"They ruined all of her hard work. She was painting things for the horses."

That didn't sound like Frankie. She was always calm and patient.

"They put hand prints all over the stable."

"And they painted Jane."

It still didn't sound right. "And that made Aunty Frankie cry?"

"And she yelled. Noah said she was really loud."

Louise interrupted. "OK, girls, go do your teeth. Then you can read to Uncle Sebastian."

They jumped up and ran off. Louise turned the phone so I could see her. She gave me her Louise smile but it didn't reach her eyes. She brushed her blonde hair out of her face.

"Is Frankie OK?" I asked. "Did she really cry? Or are they exaggerating?"

"No, she cried alright. Mum said she was out of control."

"It doesn't seem like something she'd get upset about."

"I know. She's been different since you left."

"I wouldn't know. I haven't spoken to her."

"What? Since you left?"

"I've tried calling and texting. She never answers or replies. I thought she just needed space."

"I think she needs a lot more than space. She hardly talks to anyone. She's quiet at dinner."

"Have you spoken to her?"

"No. Yes. Well, we've tried. But she just dismisses us or gets angry."

"I thought she'd be happy there. That's where she wants to be."

"Maybe here isn't the same without you."

The twins came rushing back in. They sat on the couch with Noah and Sarah and read to me. I swear those kids only sat still when eating or books were involved. It was a funny book about a dog who always got into mischief. We all laughed at its antics. When they finished, we said goodnight.

A knock sounded on my door.

"Come in."

Edward opened the door and rested against the door jamb. "Who were you speaking to?"

How was I going to explain who they were to me? "Frankie's nieces and nephew."

"Who's Frankie?"

"A lady I met in Australia."

"And her nieces and nephew call you?" He tilted his head.

"Yes. We talk about their day and then they read to me."

He considered me. "You must be close to them."

"I am. I miss them."

"And they miss you by the sounds of it. What about Frankie?"

I stood up and crossed my arms "What about Frankie?"

"Do you miss her?"

What was with all of his questions?

"With all of my being."

There was no point lying or hiding my feelings even if I risked him reporting back to our mother. But I didn't think he would. He had never done it as a child and there was more reason then, especially when her acceptance was on the line.

His stance didn't change. He nodded slowly. Then he stepped into the room and closed the door behind him before leaning against it. "Why isn't she here with you?"

"This isn't the place for her. She would never be happy here. Frankie is..." I paced. "Frankie is a beautiful, caring person. She loves horses and the outdoors. And her family. This life would stifle her."

"And you love horses and the outdoors. And Frankie."

"Yes." What was his point?

"And you're willing to suffer this life alone. Why?"

"Because it's my duty."

He pushed himself off the door and went to the window. "But you've never wanted this, have you? Even when we were children and royal life, behaviours and expectations were being drummed into us. It never interested you."

"No. But it's not about what I want, is it?"

"Why not?" He turned to look at me.

"Are you marrying Lucinda out of duty or because you want to?"

"Oh, I very much want to. She has taught me a lot in her gentle, determined way."

I gawked at him, my mouth hanging open. That was not the answer I was expecting.

"I was angry with you for a long time. I couldn't under-stand why you weren't here, fulfilling your duty. Lucinda showed me videos of you playing polo. She shared photos with me. I'd never seen you so happy. Never here. Here you were a scrunched-up ball of despair."

I nodded. Life and love did not exist here for me.

Amazing that Lucinda could see that and show it to Edward. Those words were not something I would expect from the Edward I grew up with.

"I tried to tell our mother. But she would not let it be. She insisted this was where you belonged." He shook his head. "Lucinda was not pleased. She told me that if I was ever that cruel to our children, she would divorce me. I hadn't even proposed to her yet."

I laughed. I owed Lucinda an apology. She was much more than I ever thought she was.

"You need to leave. Before they destroy you."

"But how?"

"Lucinda has a plan."

CHAPTER FIFTY-TWO

Frankie

I SAT at the dinner table listening to the chatter absentmindedly. Sebastian's name caught my attention.

"Uncle Sebastian made scones to celebrate my reading award," Tilly said.

"He made scones? In the castle?" Mum stared at Tilly.

"Mum, show Nan the photo."

Louise brought it up on her phone and showed us all. I glanced at it and looked away. His smiling face was too much for me.

"What reading award?" I asked.

"For my improvement in reading."

"She reads to Sebastian every night," Louise explained. "It's helped with her confidence."

"How does he know about the award and I don't?"

"The girls were excited to tell him."

"Why? And why are they reading to him every night?"

"He's family," Livvy said.

I dropped my knife and fork onto the table and clenched my fists. "He's not family. He lives thousands of kilometres away."

"Distance doesn't make him less family. If you lived there with him, you'd still be our aunty," Livvy said.

Everyone watched as Livvy and I argued.

"I don't know how many times I have to tell you. I'm not leaving. This is my home."

"That could be your home if you chose it," Louise said.

"Well, I don't."

I stood up and stormed out of the house. I was tired of them all putting Sebastian up on some pedestal. He was gone. He chose not to be a part of this family. They needed to accept that.

I strode into the stable and grabbed Jane's bridle. I needed to get away from all of them and their wasted dreams.

As I turned to go to Jane's yard, I walked smack bang into my father. I took a step back and looked up at him. He smiled down at me. His strong hand reached out and stroked my hair.

"I know you're hurting. We can all see it."

I shrugged.

"Louise tells me you haven't spoken to Sebastian."

"What's the point? He left. He's there. I'm here."

"Frankie, stop being so selfish. He's there alone. You have us."

"I know, Dad." He pulled me into his arms. "I don't want him to be alone."

Dad held me tight as I continued, "I'm angry with myself for letting him go alone. How could I do that to him?"

I broke down and cried, holding onto him like he was the only thing that would stop me from falling apart.

"It's alright, kiddo."

"It's not alright. I was too scared to go with him. I was too selfish, thinking about the dream I was going to leave behind."

"Sometimes you need to make new dreams."

"I told him I would support him no matter what decision he made. But what support have I given him? Nothing."

I sobbed like a child.

"It's not too late to start."

"If he chooses to stay there, I'll need to go."

"I know. I wouldn't expect anything less."

He took the bridle from my hand and kissed my forehead. I rushed back to the house. I needed to speak to Sebastian. I sat on my bed and stared at the phone screen. I let out a shaky breath. This was the most important phone call I'd ever make and I was both relieved and scared to be making it. I dialled his number.

His phone rang.

And rang.

All the way to his message bank.

When Sebastian's voice instructed me to leave a message I was lost. I croaked out, "Sebastian, it's me. I'm sorry. I'm sorry for being selfish and leaving you there alone. I want to be with you, wherever you are. I love you."

I'D SPENT the night tossing and turning. Sebastian wouldn't have called or texted last night because of the time difference. It would be evening there now. I wanted to speak to him. I wanted to say those words to him while he listened on the other end of the line, so he knew I meant them.

I was finishing my breakfast when Louise called me into the loungeroom. Everyone was sitting around looking at the television. Louise approached me and took my hand.

"What's going on?"

"Sebastian said we should watch the engagement. He's giving a speech."

CHAPTER FIFTY-THREE

Sebastian

Lucinda approached me and adjusted my bowtie. She was scrupulous and I was sure her plan was going to work. It had to. The only thing that could fail us was the unpredictability of humans. But like Lucinda said, my mother's pride was more than predictable. I took hold of Lucinda's hand. Mine had a slight shake.

"Thank you."

"I should be thanking you. It was you who made me realise Edward was the man for me. It was his love for you that was the deciding factor; the way his anger turned to understanding."

I thought I had so much more to be thankful for. She would give me my future, if it went to plan.

"Ready?"

I nodded and strode onto the stage in the castle's ballroom. I studied the crowd. They were conversing amongst themselves. I glanced at the chandeliers, the muted murals painted on the walls, the gilded columns. The fact that it was beautiful did not escape me, but it was not my kind of beauty.

I looked towards the wings where Edward and Lucinda waited with my parents. Lucinda held Edward's hand and they both stood resolute. Just that pose alone made me feel confident we'd made the right decision for everyone involved. They were the epitome of strength.

I turned my attention back to the guests. "Thank you all for coming tonight to join the engagement celebration for my brother Prince Edward and Lady Lucinda."

I tried not to look at my mother as she walked onto the stage with my father. She believed this speech was me succumbing to my duty. In a way what I was doing was out of duty. But it had never been done in the history of our country.

I reached up to tug at my bowtie, but clenched my hand instead and returned it to my side. Sweat pooled in my underarms. I was grateful the suit hid it. Taking a deep breath, I thought of Frankie.

"I know the love they share is as strong as the love they have for Oleander. Love for this country and my family is something I share."

I could do this. I wet my lips and recalled the words I had practiced.

"It is because of this love for you that I have decided to abdicate the throne."

Murmurs made their way around the ballroom. I glanced at Edward who nodded. I hoped Frankie was watching. It wasn't finished yet. Not yet. The words meant nothing. Not unless my mother...

Breathe. Just breathe. "When the time comes, Edward will

excel in his role as king. He has already proven himself both politically and in his sovereignty. With the blessing of our King and Queen, please raise your glasses to our future monarchs."

All eyes turned to my parents. This was it. This moment would determine my future.

My mother played her part perfectly. With a smile plastered to her face she invited Edward and Lucinda to her side, turned to the guests and raised her glass. As the room erupted with applause, I slipped away from the podium and down into a dark hall. Footsteps sounded behind me. I turned to face my mother.

"Very strategic move you orchestrated."

I pulled at my bowtie untying it. "I think it's for the best. Edward will make a far better king than I would."

"What will you do now?"

"I'll return to my family in Australia."

"That's a wise decision."

She returned to the ballroom without another word. No, I love you. No wishes of good luck. No questions about my Australian family. I made my way up to my room, eager to speak to Frankie. I'd listened to her message repeatedly during the day. It was time to speak to her. The phone rang once before she answered it.

"Sebastian."

"Hi, Frankie."

"Nice speech."

"I thought so."

There was a lot of talking in the background. They must have all watched together.

"When are you coming home?" she asked.

"Make it quick, lover boy. We can't stand miserable Frankie anymore," Billy called out.

"As soon as I can book a flight."

"Come on, Frankie, tell him you love him."

"Will you shut up? He won't want to come back if he has to put up with you."

"Sure he will. He knows I'll be the best brother-in-law he'll ever have."

I imagined Frankie rolling her eyes as she said, "As if."

"Are you going to tell him or not? Some of us have work to do," Brady said.

"Is nothing sacred around here?"

"No." A chorus of voices called.

She huffed.

I smiled.

"Fine. I love you, Sebastian."

"I love you too, Frankie. I'll be home soon."

CHAPTER FIFTY-FOUR

Frankie

It was taking forever for the flight to unload. I shifted from foot to foot.

What was taking so long? It was a private flight. I watched the doors as they opened, revealing Sebastian walking out with two cases behind him. I ran towards him as a smile spread across his face. He let the cases go and took me in his arms.

"I've missed you so much. Home wasn't the same without you." I held him tight.

He kissed my hair. "I've missed you too." His lips kissed their way to mine. The warmth of them, the familiarity, the hint of coffee, was perfect. Our lips separated and he rested his forehead against mine.

"I wish my wife would greet me like that," a deep voice said. I opened my eyes to see the pilot pat Sebastian on the shoulder on his way past.

"Come on, let's go," I said. "It's too late to drive home. I've booked a room."

It *was* too late, the flight had come in at midnight, but that was not the only reason for booking a room. I wanted Sebastian to myself for just one night.

"Great idea." He pulled me in for a quick kiss.

We made our way to the airport motel. As we entered the room, I said, "I have something for you."

"The only thing I need is you."

"I think you'll like it," I said, running my hand down his chest.

Sebastian grinned. "Oh yeah?"

I pushed him onto the bed. "Sit and wait."

I walked into the bathroom and took a deep breath. How would he react? After a minute, and with my heart beating fast, I walked out into the room. Sebastian stood up as soon as he saw me in my black lace bra and knickers, his mouth hanging open. My nervousness lifted, even as my stomach did its familiar Sebastian lurch.

"I like it," he said when I stood before him.

He tangled his hand in my hair and pulled me towards him. Our mouths parted on contact and his tongue searched out mine. I drew away and rested my hand on his chest.

"I'm not finished yet." I grabbed the hem of his t-shirt and pulled it over his head. My hands ran over his wide shoulders. My eyes followed them the whole way, drinking him in. I drifted my hand down his smooth chest, my need for him burning brighter the lower it got. Over his belly and lower still. His breath hitched. My hand found his button and zip, undoing them in slow, precise movements. I kissed my way down his chest and stomach as I pulled his pants down, leaving his underwear on. His dick was already hard. I rubbed it and drew my eyes up to his face. I pushed him down into a sitting position on the bed and pulled his pants off.

"Now we're even," I said.

"Not quite." His fingers found the band of my bra. "I don't know whether to take it off or leave it on."

His eyes roved across my body while I stood in front of him. Wherever his finger trailed my skin tingled. The adoration in his eyes emboldened me. I straddled him and pushed myself against his hardness. I was already wet. His low moan as I ground against him set me on fire. I claimed his lips, parting them with my own and my tongue entered his warmth. I ground slowly, sinking further down so his dick rubbed against my sensitive nub. My stomach met his in a slow beat while my heart crashed in my chest in a tribal rhythm.

"Reminds me of the dam," he said. "Just these flimsy bits of material separating us."

His hand found my breasts and teased my nipples through the lace. Our lips separated and his found my neck. He nibbled, licked and sucked. I rubbed against him harder. My stomach tightened. His hands tightened.

"Frankie, I'm so close."

His voice, the desperation in it, drove me on. I was ready to come but I didn't want to go there without him. I clenched my teeth. Sebastian's hands dropped to my waist and he ground against me. I let go. My body spasmed, the intensity so high it was a mixture of pleasure and raw release as I came in the exact same moment Sebastian did.

I fell against his chest. Our sweat mingled as he held me tight. His shaky breath against my neck slowed.

"I've never done that before," he said. His arms were tight around me. I could feel the pool of wetness between our legs.

"Me either."

He let out a chuckle and I joined him. Our hearts had regulated themselves and I could no longer feel his thumping against my chest.

"I want you for the rest of my days, Frankie."

"You have me."

EPILOGUE

FRANKIE LAY ON THE GROUND, her enormous belly pointing up to the sky. Our three-year-old twins knelt beside her with Noah and Sarah. Noah looked each of them in the eyes. He lifted his voice in encouragement. "Are we ready?"

"Wait for me," Isabella, our four-year-old, shouted as she leapt from the bottom step and came running.

Frankie closed her eyes against the bright sun. They hadn't even touched her yet and she was giggling in anticipation.

"OK," Noah called out as if addressing a crowd. "The only way to save this beached whale is to roll her back in the water." He stood up and pointed to the blue tarp. "Two or three rolls should do it." He knelt back down. "Are we ready?"

"Yes," the children chorused.

"Roll."

They rolled Frankie onto her side. She cushioned her stomach. She wasn't making it easy for them. I didn't blame her in her state. But that's what the fear of missing out does to you. You could be 37 weeks pregnant with twins and volunteer yourself to be a beached whale.

"Roll."

The children pushed again. Frankie rolled onto her elbows and knees, protecting her huge stomach. There was no way they could roll her otherwise. She flopped onto her other side. Billy had his phone out, recording the whole thing, roaring with laughter. Brady was on the other end of the line doing the same. She was close to the tarp now. One more push would do it.

"Roll," Noah shouted.

The kids pushed her and she landed on the tarp. I breathed a sigh of relief. Until a pool of water formed under her.

Frankie laughed until tears rolled down her face.

"I don't know what you're laughing about," I said as I went to help her up.

She studied my face closely as she spoke. "I don't think we're going to make it to the hospital."

"What?" I stepped back.

"Shit," Billy said. It was the first time I'd ever heard panic in his voice.

I peered at the myriad of kids around us.

"Noah, I need you to go get Nan. Tell her Aunty Frankie is having the babies. Sarah, I need you to take the younger children closer to the house. I don't want them to be scared."

I turned to Frankie. "We need to move you inside."

"Just move the tarp to the shade. We might as well have them out here."

"True. It will be less mess," Billy said, helping his sister up.

"It's not sterile out here."

"Never killed a foal or calf," Billy replied.

"We should have stopped at three," I said, shaking my head.

"You said you wanted eight," Frankie gasped, as Billy helped her walk across the yard.

"Maybe that was ambitious."

Billy glared at me like I was crazy. "I'll tell you what's ambitious, mentioning it right now."

"What?"

When they both gave me the death stare it dawned on me. I chuckled. Yeah, right, it would be my hand she was squeezing as she pushed those babies out.

Frankie and Billy stopped. He held her upright as a contraction hit her.

"How long have you been having contractions?" I asked as I lay the tarp in the shade. This was a bad, bad idea.

"A couple of hours."

"What?" Billy and I said in unison.

"I thought we had plenty of time."

"This isn't your first time around the block. You know it gets quicker each time," Billy said.

"Yeah. Well..."

He shook his head. I helped him lower her.

"Jeez, you're heavy," he said.

He was lucky she was in the middle of a contraction.

Mum came rushing over with towels and pillows. The children moved closer.

"Don't come too close, Noah. Aunty Frankie might yell and you could get frightened."

"Like the time she yelled at us and she told us there would never be another obstacle course?" Noah asked.

"Or when she yelled at us because we painted the stable?" Sarah asked.

Brady, who was still on the other end of the phone, laughed.

"For Pete's sake, you yell at children once and they remind you for the rest of your life," Frankie said, resting back against the pillows.

"Twice," Billy corrected her.

I grinned. I loved this crazy family.

"Are you sure there's not enough time to get to the hospital?" Dad asked as he hopped off the tractor he'd parked close by. "Twins are tricky."

Frankie looked at me. "Sebastian, you need to take my underwear off. I need to push."

That's all the answer we needed.

"Jim, I need you to go get the strong scissors, the ones we cut the chicken with. Disinfect them. We need them to cut the umbilical cord. Find something to clamp on the cords as well," Margaret said.

He strode past the children, who were glued to their spots. I pulled Frankie's dress up out of the way and pulled off her underwear, lifting each foot through the leg holes.

"OK. I'm outta here," Billy said.

Mum glared at him. "You can't go. You need to hold a baby while the other one is delivered."

"OK, well, I'll just stay up the head end."

Frankie's eyes were closed, her teeth clenched.

"What's happening?" Brady asked over the phone.

"Having...baby..." Frankie gasped out.

"Yeah, I know that. But what's happening right now?"

"Having..."

"Oh shit."

"How can we tell if they're in the right position?" I asked.

"They've been head down for weeks. It's likely they still are." Mum positioned herself between Frankie's legs.

Frankie's breaths rushed out as she pushed.

"You're doing great," I said as she squeezed my hand. Hard.

She clenched her teeth and pushed again. Minutes went on by. Dad arrived with the scissors.

"Geez, you're nearly as quiet as a cow," Billy remarked.

Brady mooed.

Frankie shot Billy a look and eyed the phone camera in Billy's hands to do the same to Brady.

"OK, one big push and I think the baby will be out," Mum said.

Frankie moaned long and hard as she pushed. I glanced at the children, who stood wide-eyed. Faint crying brought my attention back to Frankie.

"A girl," Mum said. She and dad wrapped the baby, cut the cord and handed it to Billy.

Frankie leant back against the pillows. She smiled as I bent down to kiss her. "You're doing great. Have a rest while you can."

She nodded. I looked up at Billy as he knelt beside us, holding our baby. He couldn't take his eyes off her. "She has your hair, Frankie. Look at it all." He handed the baby to her. I stared at our marvellous creation and kissed Frankie again.

"Perfect. Just like you."

She rested deeper against the pillows and I took the baby, holding it close and smoothing its wet hair. I kissed her on the forehead before handing her back to Billy. He walked over to the waiting crowd and knelt down so they could all have a look. Louise was there too and she explained the blood and mucous to the children.

Frankie tensed. Her eyes opened and I saw the determination there as she pushed.

"Good girl, Frankie, nearly there."

Frankie rested between pushes, her breath escaping in gasps. I held her hand tight as her whole upper body tensed.

"Just a bit more, Frankie."

Frankie didn't have the energy for just a bit more. She flopped down on the pillows.

"It's OK. It will come with the next one." I wiped the wet hair off her face.

She nodded, sucked a breath in and pushed. Mum laughed when the baby landed in her waiting hands. As soon as they cut the cord, she handed the baby to me. "Another girl."

I smiled and handed the baby to Frankie. "Three girls and two boys. We'll have to go for at least one more to even it up."

Frankie reached up and pulled me towards her. My lips met hers, relishing in their familiarity. As she drew away, she said, "Just one more."

THANK YOU for reading my novel.

To be notified of future releases, and to keep up to date with other news, please join my newsletter.
https://www.subscribepage.com/p9p9yo

BOOK REVIEWS from awesome readers like you are the lifeblood of authors, especially new authors. Reviews help readers find new books and authors find new readers. They don't need to be long or detailed, even two sentence reviews add value.

It would be appreciated if you could leave a review here:

Amazon

Goodreads

BookBub

IF YOU WOULD LIKE to watch a video of the Nutbush dance you can check it out here: https://youtu.be/qHqzjQty7aY

OTHER books available in the Love Down Under Series are:

Let Sleeping Dogs Lie

When she left him…

…Tara couldn't explain why.

After five years, did she still have feelings for Shepherd?

Her brother's passing hit Tara hard and it left a scar. That night, at the party, when she saw Shepherd high, Tara had no choice, it was over. It brought up too many painful memories and she wouldn't go through it again. The decision was simple.

She had to leave.

No goodbye.

For Shepherd, losing Tara broke his heart. Not knowing why she left, well that pain he addressed with drugs, alcohol, and meaningless relationships. After he hit rock bottom, he cleaned up and came up with a plan to get her back. Could it work?

It was his only shot.

Would a desperate ruse, with the best intentions, but costing a fortune, give him the chance to win her heart for good? Or would it ruin him?

Will she be brave enough to be loved?

The Cat's Out of the Bag

She started a new life …

…he's escaping his.

Can two tortured souls find a future together?

Evie's a survivor. After rebuilding herself and her life, she's feeling the one thing she never thought she would – happy.

Until Jesse...

When she meets Jesse while volunteering at a cat shelter, dark memories of her past return. She is stronger now and wants to trust him, but after all she's been through, is trust even possible?

Jesse's a self-made billionaire yearning to get away from his empty life and the money-hungry parasites who inhabit it.

The plan?

Go to sunny Australia, leaving his old life behind, to find himself. But instead of finding just himself, he finds Evie, who is everything anyone should aspire to be. Now, what he aspires to be, is hers.

But to be hers, he needs to tell her everything. The only thing holding him back is his fear of finding out she's just another parasite.

The quest to find a cat a forever home leads them to travel across the country together. Will they find the strength to confide in each other? Or will the close quarters drive them apart?

Have you ever had a best friend you loved? But never pursued them because you knew they had a better life to live?

Emily and Luke were those best friends. They lived next door to each other for eighteen years, spending every spare moment together. Then Emily went to university and Luke took over the family farm.

Now, Emily has returned to care for her estranged father. She has no intention of staying longer than needed and prepares the farm for sale.

Her progressive ways cause the local farming co-op to distrust her, and they pressure Luke into finding out what she's up to. He agrees, to keep them off Emily's back. It's not like it would be hard; they shared everything with each other, anyway.

Before Luke knows what's happening, he's not only spying on Emily, but he's dating her, too.

So begins a case of fake dating where they're likely to lose the most precious thing of all, each other.

ACKNOWLEDGMENTS

Cover by Charmaine Ross Cover Designs
Edited by Salt & Sage Books
Proofread by Claerie Kavanagh
And thanks to my amazing beta readers

ABOUT THE AUTHOR

Cynthia is a project officer by day and a writer by night. She enjoys writing about places she visited with her daughter while they travelled around Australia. She says that travel and reading are the best educators. Still, to this day, they both enjoy travelling and reading. A love of animals sees them feature in her books, some have small parts, others larger.

Find her online: http://cynthiaterelst.com/

All of her social links can be found here, Linktree: https://linktr.ee/cynthiaterelst